Starlight's Shooting Star

The Starlight Series
Book Four

in which Miranda and her friends
encounter many more adventures
and learn more of life's lessons;
and in which a special baby is born:
a tiny foal that plays a large part in
granting Miranda's biggest wishes.

Other Books in the *Starlight Series* by Janet Muirhead Hill

Book 1: **Miranda and Starlight**: "A heartfelt story with a main character who is feisty and energetic. Young readers need more good horse books like this one."
   -- *Nora Martin,* author of *The Eagles Shadow, The Stone Dancers,* and *A perfect Storm.*

Book 2: "**Starlight's Courage** is a must read for any young lady who loves horses. Though it is the second book in the Starlight series, Starlight's Courage is a great read on it's own. Hill successfully tackles serious issues facing today's youth in a comfortable manner making the book not only entertaining, but also educational."
   -- *Sterling Pearce / GWN Reviewer*

Book 3: "**Starlight, Star Bright** is perfect for anyone age eight or up who loves horses. It is clearly written out in a way young readers can easily understand and relate to. This is one exceptional series! *****
   -- *Huntress Reviews* (Reviewed by *Detra Fitch*)

And this one, Book 4: **Starlight's Shooting Star,** an exciting and magical additon to a series in which "beautiful black and white illustrations by Pat Lehmkuhl enhance Janet Muirhead Hill's charming and highly recommended story for young readers."
   --*Children's Bookwatch*

Starlight's Shooting Star

Janet Muirhead Hill

Illustrated by
Pat Lehmkuhl

Raven Publishing

Starlight's Shooting Star

by
Janet Muirhead Hill

Published by:
Raven Publishing
PO Box 2885
Norris, Montana 59745
e-mail: info@ravenpublishing.net

Printed in the USA

ISBN: 0-9714161-3-3 3339 9253 $^{10}/_{05}$
Library of Congress Control Number: 2003091205

For
Dorothy Elkins Muirhead

Thanks, Mom, for unconditional love,
encouragement, and faith in me.

Acknowledgments:

Thanks to all who helped with editing: Florence Ore, the
Harrison High School Creative writing class, 2003, Joan
Bochmann, Shirley Wertz, Sharon Beall, Denise Sarrazin,
Tayla Andrews, Jayme Schaak, Jan Zimmerman, and to all
others who read the manuscript and gave me advice.
Thanks to Doctor David Catlin and to Tracy Tess for techni-
cal consultation on the medical issues in the book.
Thanks to my husband, Stan Hill and other family members,
friends and fans who continue to believe in me.
Thanks especially to the kids who have sent letters and
e-mails to tell me how you like my books.

Chapter One

Miss Marigold Hopper stood before the twelve students of the sixth grade class on the first day of school. To Miranda Stevens, this pretty young teacher, fresh out of college, seemed vivacious, intelligent, and disciplined. It looked like it would be a fun but orderly school year.

"We are all here to learn," Miss Hopper said that Wednesday morning, "and you will help set the atmosphere for learning. You will make the rules for class conduct and I will lead you in an adventure of discovery. We won't follow the text books, but together we will develop a lesson plan that will challenge your minds and hold your interest."

She asked them to suggest rules, writing them on the board as they shouted them out. They were the usual: be courteous, respect the teacher, respect each other's feelings, don't steal, don't lie, be on time. Miss Hopper added a few of her own: turn in your homework on time; if you have questions, ask the teacher, not each other; no talking during tests.

"I think I'm going to like the new teacher," Miranda told her friends, Laurie Langley and Christopher Bergman at lunch time.

"I don't know," said Chris. "She sounds awfully strict to me."

"I can handle that if she makes classes interesting," Miranda said.

"Yeah, right," Chris said, his freckled face breaking into a teasing grin, "I can't even imagine it. Obedient little Miranda saying, 'yes, teacher, whatever you say, teacher.'"

Chris pretended to toss a pony tail over his shoulder and then ran his fingers through the short, red curls on top of his head. Miranda laughed.

"Sounds to me like we'll have lots of field trips and some fun assignments," Laurie said, her brown eyes sparkling.

"Are you going to Shady Hills after school?" Miranda asked her friends.

Chris had to help his dad stock shelves in their store. Laurie's father was coming home for dinner, and she had to help her mother prepare. It was always a big occasion when he returned from a sales trip.

Before afternoon classes began, Miranda called home to ask her grandmother if she could ride the bus to Shady Hills Horse Ranch with Elliot, Mr. Taylor's seven-year-old grandson. Seeing her black stallion, Starlight, was the high point of Miranda's life, and she never missed a chance to be with him. Well, he was half hers, which was more than she had ever allowed herself to hope for.

Grandma didn't answer the phone. She was probably working outside, or maybe she had gone to the store. Miranda tried again after school.

"No, come home on your own bus," Grandma told Miranda. "Corey and Jolene have come to help Grandpa put up the new machine shed. You can watch Cody so Jolene and I can help."

Miranda ran to the bus just as it was pulling away from the curb.

"Wait!" she shouted, waving her arms.

But no one heard, and no one looked back to see her. She dashed back into the school and tried to call Grandma again. There was no answer. Miranda began the long walk home.

She had lived with her grandparents long enough that it seemed more like home than any of the apartments where she had lived with her mother in California. It had been hard to come to a new school at first, but now she didn't ever want to go back to the big schools in the city. She hoped she would never have to leave her grandparent's dairy farm.

It took her an hour to walk the three miles home. She had hoped someone might come to meet her when they saw the bus go by without stopping, but no one did. As she neared the driveway, a big black, bear-like creature came bounding toward her. She braced herself to keep from being bowled over.

"Hi, Bro. At least someone is glad to see me," Miranda said, petting his big head affectionately.

Little Brother was the puppy she'd found whimpering near the county road less than three months ago. It was hard to believe he'd ever been the tiny ball of fur she'd easily held in her small hands. And he was still growing. Judging from his size, shape and thick black coat, Grandpa guessed he was a Newfoundland-Labrador cross.

She walked past the garage and the granary to where a big metal building was being erected. Her Aunt Jolene was just taking a sleepy toddler from the car parked nearby.

"He just woke up from his nap, Miranda," said her aunt. "Will you take him in the house and change him? He can have a snack. I left some arrowroot cookies and some apple juice in the kitchen."

"Come to cousin, Cody," Miranda said, smiling. "We'll go have some fun."

Cody smiled as he held out his arms to her. Since Corey, Jolene, and Cody lived in Kalispell, Miranda didn't see them often, but Cody never seemed to forget her. They had a good time together, and Miranda watched him every minute as they played.

Miranda went to school the next morning, hoping the day would pass quickly so she could soon ride Starlight. The teacher seemed a little less confident, today, referring to notes on her desk as she gave out assignments and talked about possible activities for the future. Most of the time, she just talked about herself, her college experiences, and what she didn't agree with in the traditional school system. Not until the first period after lunch did she give them anything concrete to work on.

"By the end of this quarter, you will each turn in a twenty page paper which will include footnotes, a complete bibliography of at least six sources, and a title page. It must be typed or printed on a word processor." When the students groaned, Miss Hopper added, "You have almost nine weeks to complete this project, and you may choose any topic that interests you, as long as I approve it. I will be pretty lenient on topics as long as it isn't something completely trivial."

When Miranda asked to research and write about the history of horse racing, Miss Hopper said no, that subject was too trivial. How to train a horse was also vetoed.

"Then what isn't trivial?" Miranda asked.

"Write about something scientific, a great moment in world history, another culture, or a career."

"Horse racing is a career. Horse training is a career!" Miranda had argued. "Don't you know anything?"

"Miss Stevens. You will not talk to me with disrespect. For that you get two days of detention. Report to the library for an hour after school today and tomorrow."

Sixth grade was off to an unhappy beginning after all. For Miranda, there could be no worse punishment than keeping her away from her horse. A seed of contempt for Miss Hopper had been sown in Miranda's heart.

Grandma didn't allow Miranda to go to Shady Hills Horse Ranch after detention on Thursday or Friday. But on Saturday morning, Grandma agreed to let her go as soon as she finished her chores. Miranda, determined to make it up to Starlight by getting there as early as possible, was up before dawn, doing chores and getting ready. She intended to spend two long days with him before she had to go back to school on Monday. Grandma drove her to the stables after an early breakfast. To Miranda's surprise, a faded red Honda sedan with a rumpled fender and cracked windshield was parked in front of Mr. Taylor's two car garage.

"Looks like Mr. Taylor has company," said Grandma.

"I wonder who. It doesn't look like the sort of company Mr. Taylor would invite to his house," said Miranda.

In fact, she'd never known the elderly owner of Shady Hills to have visitors in his sprawling ranch house. Though she had learned he could be generous and kindhearted, his stern and often grouchy demeanor kept him from being particularly well liked. Seeing signs of a visitor so early in the morning filled her with curiosity. She looked at the license plate on the back of the little car. It was from Kansas.

Grandma stopped in front of the stable, and Miranda jumped out.

"Thanks Gram. See you this evening," she said, grabbing her lunch and dashing to Starlight's stall, forgetting the mysterious visitor completely.

Starlight was the favored prospect for replacing Cadillac's Last Knight, Cassius Taylor's famous

Thoroughbred stallion. Knight had won his share of races before he was retired from the track to sire winning foals. People brought their mares from all over the country to the Shady Hills Horse Ranch in Montana to get a black foal from this horse who always bred true. Starlight, whose registered name was Sir

Jet Propelled Cadillac, came from a black mare named Jet Stream Dream. He was so purely black, muscular, and full of energy as a yearling, that he'd been chosen to succeed his famous sire, Last Knight.

Mr. Taylor's plans had been shaken when Miranda let the colt get away and fall into a tangle of barbed wire. The resulting wounds had almost cost the colt his life, and had certainly dashed Mr. Taylor's hopes. Determined to save this precious colt she called Starlight at any cost, Miranda nursed him back to health and won his heart in the process. When she demonstrated that Starlight could run faster than any horse Shady Hills had ever produced, even his sire in his prime, Mr. Taylor renewed his plans for making him the successor for Last Knight. Of course, he'd have to win some races first to establish a name.

After Starlight had thrown a couple of grown men, Mr. Taylor began to see that no one could get Starlight's cooperation as well as Miranda. Just when Miranda had given up hope that she would ever be able to own Starlight, Mr. Taylor made her a partner. In exchange for her cooperation in his training, Mr. Taylor signed papers that gave Miranda half interest in Sir Jet Propelled Cadillac; her Starlight.

"Starlight, I'm so sorry I didn't get to see you the past three days. I missed you," Miranda called as she ran through the stall and found Starlight grazing at the far end of his narrow paddock.

Starlight nickered, put his head down, kicked up his hind feet in a sort of twisted little jump, and trotted up to meet her. He nudged her with his nose, and she had to step backward to keep her balance. She scratched his neck and face as she reached into her pocket for a treat for him. She had found that he loved celery, so she brought several sticks of it as well as some small carrots.

"I can tell that you missed me too," she said. "Don't worry. You and I are going to spend the whole day together. First we'll play on the longe line, then maybe do some laps on the track, but as soon as Chris and Laurie get here, I'm taking you to the river pasture. Laurie's mom is coming with us, and we're having a picnic lunch. We'll make a day of it."

Starlight enjoyed working on the longe line with Miranda. It had become a game they played each day as he ran faster and faster around her as she stood in the center of a circle as wide as the longe line would allow. Then she would gradually pull him closer, until he spiraled in to stop in front of her.

The sun shone brightly and the light frost that had covered the grass that morning turned to sparkling drops. After his exercise on the longe, Miranda led Starlight to the tack shed and wrapped his lead rope around the hitching post. She brushed his glistening coat and then rubbed him down with fly wipe, before going back in to choose a saddle for the ride to the river pasture.

"I think I'll use a western saddle today," she told Starlight as she came out carrying the smallest one she could find. "It'll be something new for you."

Mrs. Langley's new car pulled up in front of the stable and Miranda's two best friends, Laurie and

Christopher, piled out.

"Hurry and get your horses ready," Miranda called. "Starlight and I are almost ready to head for the pasture. You're going to ride with us, aren't you, Mrs. Langley?"

"Yes, indeed," replied Laurie's mother. "I couldn't even be tempted to stay inside on such a glorious day. I'll go find Mr. Taylor and make sure I can rent Cinder for the day."

"Here he comes now," said Laurie. "Who's that with him?"

Miranda looked up to see a slight young man trotting along beside Mr. Taylor. This must be the visitor, she realized, hoping he wouldn't be staying long.

"Certainly. I had Adam bring him in for you last night. He's in the stall next to Lady's," Miranda heard Mr. Taylor tell Mrs. Langley.

"Would Elliot like to come with us?" Mrs. Langley asked, referring to Mr. Taylor's grandson who now lived with him. Elliot's mother had died less than a year ago in England.

"No, Elliot's going with Adam and me to Helena today, but thanks for asking." Mr. Taylor seemed in a hurry to get past Mrs. Langley, and when she stepped aside he strode toward Miranda.

"Miranda, I want you to meet Colton Spencer," Mr. Taylor said.

"Hello," she said.

She thought it strange that he introduced his visitor to her and not to Laurie's mom. Colton had a narrow, pimply face, light brown hair that looked as if it hadn't been combed, and bright blue eyes that seemed too big for his thin face.

"Colton is the young man I was telling you about, Miranda. He has come to train Sir Jet with you," Mr. Taylor explained.

"Oh," Miranda gasped. "I didn't know he was coming so soon."

In truth, Miranda had forgotten about her agreement with Mr. Taylor to work with a jockey. She was supposed to teach him to get the most out of Starlight and not get bucked off like the rider in his first race had.

"Well, here he is. He just got his license from the Montana Board of Horse racing, so he'll be able to ride in the next race."

"But there aren't any more races until spring," Miranda said, "So there isn't any hurry. I guess we could start Monday after school."

"No more races in Montana, but we can't wait until spring to get some wins to Sir Jet's name. There is a race in Denver in November," Mr. Taylor said. "We have no time to lose. I want you to start today."

"But Mr. Taylor, I was going to ride with Mrs. Langley and Laurie and Chris..."

"They'll have to get along without you," Mr. Taylor interrupted. "With you in school now, I want you to spend your weekends and evenings helping Colton."

Chapter Two

Miranda glared at the homely, awkward stranger as her friends rode toward the river pasture without her. Colton Spencer stared back for a few moments before looking at the ground. He scraped the toe of his worn cowboy boot in the dust.

"Sorry to interrupt your plans. Look, if you don't want to do this, go on with your friends. Mr. Taylor's gone now. I won't tell him," he said.

"Fine, maybe I will. I never wanted to teach a stranger how to ride my horse. But it was part of the deal. He wouldn't be even part mine if I hadn't agreed," Miranda said.

"Well, I don't exactly like to have a kid telling me how to do what I've been doing my whole life, either," Colton said, looking her in the eye.

"No, I suppose not," Miranda said in a softer tone. "So why did you come here?"

"It isn't so easy to get a job when you're first

getting started. I saw his ad in a racing journal and sent an application," Colton explained. "Of course the ad didn't mention I'd be working for a ten-year-old."

"I'm eleven and a half!" Miranda informed him. "And if you don't want to work for me, just go back to Kansas."

"Sorry, I'm stuck. It took every dime I had to get here."

"When did you get here? Did you stay with Mr. Taylor all night?" Miranda was curious.

"I got here about eight. I didn't have any place else to go. At first I thought I'd have to sleep in my car, but then he told me I could have the bedroom. He sleeps on a couch in his den," Colton said with awe in his voice. "He's kind of strange, isn't he?"

"He's okay." Miranda said. She thought Mr. Taylor was eccentric and unpredictable but she had grown to respect his right to be just the way he was. "Are you going to stay in his house until you can afford to rent a place?"

"Hey, the ad said my housing would be furnished. He's going to have to put me up. I'll stay in his house until there's room in the bunk house. Mr. Taylor said it would be two weeks."

"What? Who's moving out of the bunk house?"

Miranda was alarmed. She couldn't imagine that Higgins, the old groom and trainer, would leave. He seemed to have recovered well from his broken hip and was back to working with the horses again. Miranda had grown very fond of him.

"I don't know. You'll have to ask Mr. Taylor, I

guess," Colton said, "Shall we get started, or are you going to catch up with your friends?"

Miranda stared at Colton's long thin nose which turned up at the end. *He looks like Pinnochio*, she thought. She had no idea how or what she was supposed to teach this young jockey. She decided she'd have to see what he knew about horses. If he believed as Adam Barber did, that man was master and a horse must submit, it might be a hopeless case. She believed that Starlight and all horses were born free spirits, and would only do their best for a human if it was their own choice. Starlight was easy for her to ride and train because there was a bond of love and understanding between them.

"I'm going to put Starlight back in his paddock. I'll watch while you catch him," Miranda said, leading Starlight back to the paddock.

"Why do you want to do that? You think I don't know how to catch a horse? I grew up with horses, I'll have you know!" Colton exclaimed angrily.

"Not Starlight," Miranda said.

She handed Colton the halter, climbed up on the fence and then onto the roof of the stable. She sat with her arms around her knees, out of Starlight's sight but with a good view of the whole paddock.

"This is stupid. I don't like having a little girl watching me like a hawk," Colton grumbled.

Miranda shrugged and waited for him to begin. Shaking his head, Colton put the halter behind his back and walked toward Starlight. Starlight stared at Colton as he approached. Just as the young man reached out to touch him, Starlight arched his neck, pivoted and ran to the end of the paddock. With a deep sigh and a glance at Miranda, Colton turned and followed the horse. The routine was repeated at the far end of the paddock, and Starlight ran back toward the stable. Colton saw his chance to trap him in his stall. He ran behind him, but when Starlight got to the open door, he turned to face Colton.

"Hey yaaah!" Colton shouted, waving his arms and the halter.

Starlight, snorted, pranced, and dashed along the fence past Colton to the far end of the paddock. Miranda couldn't help laughing. When she saw Colton looking at her she tried to stop.

"All right, Smarty," Colton said. "I suppose you can do better. I'll get him. I just have to wear him down. He'll get tired pretty soon."

"I wouldn't count on him getting tired before you do. This is a game to him, and he's loving it."

"Then get me a lariat and I'll rope him."

"Over my dead body!" Miranda exclaimed, climbing off the roof. "You have to gain his confidence. Let him get to know you. But if you hurt him or scare him, I'll make sure you get fired."

"So what do you want me to do? Play cat and mouse with him all day?" Colton asked angrily. "I could be riding him if you hadn't turned him loose. That's what I was hired to do, you know."

"So far, I'm the only person who has ridden Starlight without being bucked off," Miranda said. "I wish I could keep it that way, but they won't let me ride him in a race because I'm not old enough. But Mr. Taylor has seen what Starlight will do for me. That's why he wants me to teach you how I do it. If you don't like it, quit."

Colton looked as if he'd like to strangle her. She forced herself to keep looking him in the eye, determined not to let him see that she felt like crying. As she watched him fight for control of his anger, his expression suddenly changed. He smiled and threw up his hands.

"Okay, boss," he said softly. "What do I do now?"

"I'll leave you alone with him while I go clean some stalls," Miranda said. "Take your time. Talk to him. Get to know him and let him get to know you. And don't bother about trying to hide the halter from him. He's not stupid."

Miranda went into his stall and closed the door behind her. When she finished cleaning his stall, she cleaned Queen's and Lady's as fast as she could, mainly to keep her feelings at bay. But when the work was done she slumped into the corner of Lady's stall and cried.

"Starlight," she whispered between sobs, "if I don't help Colton win your trust, I'll be letting Mr. Taylor down. But if I do, you aren't all mine anymore."

She finally stood, wiped her nose and eyes on her shirt sleeve, and quietly climbed up on the stable roof. She saw Colton sitting on the ground in the corner of the paddock. Starlight had his head down, almost in Colton's lap getting his face patted and his ears scratched. She watched as Colton stood up slowly, still petting Starlight.

"I've got to hand it to you, Miranda," Colton said with a huge grin on his face as he spotted her on the roof. "I've learned something new today. Who taught you?"

Miranda was surprised by the question. She had never thought about it.

"Starlight, I guess. It just makes sense to treat an animal like you'd like to be treated. I love Starlight with all my heart and he loves me back."

"So, what do we do next," asked Colton.

"Well, I always longe him before I ride."

"Why?"

"To warm him up. I know there are other ways. Adam used the exercise wheel. But longeing is like a game for Starlight and me."

She bit her tongue, wishing she hadn't even mentioned it. She'd rather keep her play time with Starlight to herself.

"We did that before you came out this morning, so I guess we're ready to saddle him," she said.

Miranda rode first, using the bitless bridle that she preferred. Colton had never seen such a thing and said he'd never get away with using that in a real race. He followed Miranda down the hill past the old barn to the oval race track.

"Let me show you what he can do, and then I'll let you try."

Colton frowned but didn't argue. As she trotted around the race track, she thought only of her horse, of how much she loved feeling like she was a part of him as he responded to her slightest cues. She sat totally relaxed when she started out. Starlight responded with a smooth easy jog and then stretched out into a lope. She patted his withers softly and leaned over his neck.

"Good boy, Starlight."

He picked up the pace and she felt like they were flying. She could hardly feel his hooves touching the ground. They made two laps around the track at this speed. She saw Colton get down from the fence as she approached the third time around. Instead of slowing down, she raised up in the saddle, her face in

Starlight's flowing black mane.

"Okay, boy. Now you can run."

The sudden burst of speed took her breath away as it always did. The wind in her face brought tears to her eyes. This was flying. This was ecstacy.

Colton's face was full of surprise and admiration when they finally stopped in front of him.

"I never saw a horse run so fast in my life!" he exclaimed. "I thought you had him going as fast as you could the second time around the track. What stamina! Why he isn't even breathing hard. I never saw anything like it."

Miranda didn't let Colton ride yet.

"Here, lead him around the track to cool him down. Talk to him as you go. You have time to get better acquainted before you get on."

Reluctant to give up her horse, she stayed on his back as she handed Colton the reins. Colton didn't argue.

The phone rang just as Miranda was getting into bed that night. Somehow she knew it was her mother before she answered.

"Hi, Sweetie. How's it going?" her mother asked.

"Pretty good. I wish school hadn't started and there is a new guy at Shady Hills," Miranda began.

"Did you see Adam, today?" her mother asked.

"No, why?"

"I need to talk to him and I haven't been able to reach him."

"He went with Mr. Taylor to Helena. Why?"

Miranda's mood darkened. Her mother wasn't really interested in Miranda; she only called to find out about Adam Barber, her fiance. Adam had come to Shady Hills as a riding instructor for her friend, Christopher, but had stayed on to work for Mr. Taylor when his elderly groom and trainer, Higgins, was injured. Miranda had never liked Adam, handsome as he was, for he either ignored her or treated her like a baby. It was through him, however, that she learned that her father had been lost at sea when he attempted to save another sailor. Adam had gone on to California to tell her mother this news. To Miranda's horror, an attraction developed between Adam and her mother, and all too soon her mother informed Miranda that she was going to marry Adam.

"Well, it's Margot," Mom explained. "She doesn't seem at all happy here, and she isn't doing well in school,"

Margot was Adam's eight-year-old daughter. When her mother died, she became Adam's responsibility, but he'd shifted that burden to Miranda's mother by leaving her in California. "So Margot can bond with her future stepmother," Adam had explained.

"Is she going to come live with Adam, then?" Miranda asked.

"No, Adam is coming here. He gave Mr. Taylor two weeks notice, but I think he shouldn't wait that long. His daughter needs him now."

Chapter Three

So that's who was moving out of the bunk-house. Miranda would have been glad to have him gone, if only he wasn't going to be near her mother.

"Does that mean you're getting married now? Miranda asked in horror.

"No. Adam has rented an apartment nearby. He wanted me to elope with him, but I'm determined to have a real wedding in June. You'll be a part of it. Margot will be my flower girl. I can't wait for you to meet her, Miranda. You'll love having a little sister, I know you will."

Miranda wasn't so sure.

"I can't believe my eyes," Mr. Taylor told Miranda as he clocked Starlight on the track one day in early October. "He's running just as fast with Colton as he did with you — faster than Knight did when he was in his prime."

She watched Colton sit back and relax in the saddle and Starlight began to slow. They rounded the track once before stopping in front of Mr. Taylor.

"That horse is ready, and so are you, I think," Mr. Taylor said to Colton. "Have you always ridden like that?"

"I probably would have made the same mistake as the other guys who tried to ride him, if Miranda hadn't shared her secrets with me. I'll never look at horses in the same way again. And I think I'll have much better success with them," Colton said, flashing a smile at Miranda.

"Well, between you and Miranda, I'm sure you can keep him in form." Mr. Taylor said. "Colton, I realize you signed on as a jockey, but would you like to start some coming three year olds? They should have been well broke by now, but I've been so short handed, I haven't had a chance."

"Sure," Colton answered. "I'll be glad to have more horses to work with. Miranda had all the work done on this one. I just had to learn to let him do his thing."

"I don't want you getting hurt so that you can't ride. I can't afford to lose a good rider. Be careful, and if they give you any trouble, I'll find someone to break them first."

"Did you hear that?" Miranda asked Colton when Mr. Taylor went back to the house. "Why do men talk about breaking horses? Do they want them broken? Let me help you, Colton, so he won't think he needs to hire some bronc-buster."

"Sure, Miranda," Colton said.

After Adam left, Colton not only settled into the bunk house with Higgins, but gradually took on more and more of the chores. Higgins was back to work again after being laid up with a broken hip for several months. But Mr. Taylor didn't allow him to do any of the heavy work, like mucking stalls or carrying bales of hay. Higgins spent most of his time keeping track of all the horses on the ranch and making sure the breeding, health care, and when possible, the training was on schedule. Colton, who had come to regard Miranda as an equal, told her everything that went on in the bunk house and his routine.

Miranda was no longer jealous of Colton's ability to ride Starlight and get his cooperation. It was plain he wasn't trying to take her place in his affections. She spent some of her time helping Colton with other horses, but always made sure she didn't neglect Starlight. And Starlight made it plain that seeing Miranda was the highlight of his day. Every moment spent at Shady Hills was happy. The same could not be said about school.

"Quiet!" yelled Miss Hopper, but no one but Miranda seemed to hear her over the din.

"Shut up!" she screamed, slamming a book on her desk for attention.

Finally, the room fell silent.

"Everyone line up against the back wall," she demanded. "Now, when I call your name, come and take the seat I'm pointing to."

From her grade book, she read the names of her twelve pupils alphabetically. Starting at the front of the first row of four desks, she pointed to one desk after another as the students came to her call. Miranda sat next to the back of the third row, Laurie was at the front of the middle row, and Chris sat second from the front of the first row. The class was quiet as they stared at the teacher. Her face was red and her mouth pressed in a hard thin line.

"I want order in the classroom. If you are going to behave like first graders, I'll treat you like first graders!" she shouted. "No one speak without raising your hand and don't get out of your desk without permission."

"What got into her?" Miranda asked Laurie at recess.

"I heard she got called into Mr. Alderman's office. My mom went to see him last week to complain about her, and he said he'd had some similar complaints from other parents and teachers."

"At the parent-teacher conferences last week, Grandma told her that I said it was impossible to study in there anymore. Miss Hopper acted like she didn't know what Gram was talking about."

"My mom complained, too, but it didn't change anything," Laurie said.

"What do you suppose happened? At the beginning she talked like she would be strict and cover so much material. She said we wouldn't follow books, but she's not doing anything," Miranda complained.

Four other girls from their class joined the conversation.

"She has a boyfriend," Lisa informed them.

"Yeah," Kimberly said. "It's my cousin, Jeb. That's why she is so nice to me. She wants to talk about him all the time."

"Don't blame Kimberly if it seems like she's teacher's pet," said Stephanie, "or the rest of us, just because we hang out together. It's not like any of us like to hear all the stuff she tells us."

"She tells us about her love life and then asks us about ours. She wants to know who our boyfriends are," added Tammy. "It's like she wants to be one of the kids instead of the teacher."

"She treats us like we don't exist most of the time. When the rest of us ask her something, she tells us to figure it out, like it's simple and we're stupid to be asking. I think she doesn't know the answers herself," Miranda said.

"Believe me, I'd rather she ignored me! I hate how she asks me about my cousin all the time," Kimberly said.

"How long do you think she'll keep order in the class?" Laurie asked.

"About as long as she did at the beginning of school; two or three days until we figured out she didn't mean half the stuff she said," Lisa replied.

Miranda raised her hand when everyone was back in their assigned seats after recess. For a long time, Miss Hopper didn't notice. Miranda sat stubbornly with her hand held high, until all the kids in the class were looking at her. Miss Hopper finally noticed.

"What is it, Miranda?"

"When are we going on one of the field trips you promised?"

"Field trip, well," Miss Hopper began uncertainly. "I plan to take you to some caves when we get into our section on geology."

"Let's start it now," Miranda suggested. "We aren't doing anything else in science."

Kimberly raised her hand and the teacher quickly acknowledged her.

"I think I could get my cousin, Jeb, to help out. He has a commercial driver's license so he could even drive the bus," Kimberly said.

"Well now, I think that's a great idea. Thank you Miranda and Kimberly." Miss Hopper looked relieved. "Let's go to the Lewis and Clark Caverns."

"Can't!" Bill said, not bothering to raise his hand. "It's closed for the season."

"Oh, surely not," Miss Hopper began.

"My mom works there as a guide. I know when it closes," Bill argued.

"I know where there's a cave!" Miranda shouted. "It's on private property but I'll ask permission for us to go."

Miranda felt important as she led the noisy group of sixth-graders through the pasture and up the hill to the cave the following Thursday. It was a cold but sunny day and Miranda soon shed her heavy jacket. She stopped to look back at the group as she tied it around her waist. Others were doing the same.

The exertion of hiking was enough to keep them warm. Miss Hopper and Jeb were far behind the rest, walking hand in hand. Mr. Taylor had given his permission grudgingly after making the school sign a waiver releasing him from all liability.

"Will there be plenty of adult supervision?" he had asked Miranda.

"There are only twelve kids in our class," Miranda assured him. "The teacher and at least one other adult will come. That should be plenty."

"Not if they're all like you!" Mr. Taylor had exclaimed.

Miranda hoped he was joking. By the time she reached the cave, however, she began to wonder if he was right to worry. The boys scattered in several directions, exploring various openings in the sloping walls of the big room. Some of the girls egged them on with squeals about their bravery.

"Wait for me, Josh." Stephanie said with a giggle. "Hold my hand so I don't get lost."

"Hey you guys!" Miranda called. "We'd better stay together until Miss Hopper gets here."

"Who made you the boss, Miranda?" asked Kyle as he crawled out of a narrow hole. "That one doesn't go anywhere, guys. Wait for me, Bill."

Miss Hopper finally arrived, breathless.

"Where is everybody?" Jeb asked. "Hey, come back here!"

Putting his thumb and one finger to his lips, he whistled loudly. Soon the kids came stumbling back into the main room.

"Quiet, now!" he said. "Your teacher is going to set some ground rules and give you your assignment."

"Uh, yes," Miss Potter began. "Don't anyone go off alone and don't be gone more than half an hour. Take note of anything unusual you see, like rock formations."

"Don't get lost!" Jeb added.

Each of the children had a flash light and everyone set off in groups of two or three. Chris started to go into the tall passageway on the left.

"That doesn't go anywhere, Chris," Miranda called. "Come with Laurie and me."

She led them on hands and knees through a very small opening. She had explored it far enough to know that it opened into a room big enough to stand up in, with at least two passages leading farther into the cave.

"Did you see that?" Laurie asked as she came out of the short tunnel to stand beside Chris and Miranda. "Miss Hopper and Jeb went off together into that room you said didn't go anywhere."

"It goes into a smaller room and dead ends," Miranda explained. "I used it for a bedroom when I camped out here with Starlight."

Chapter Four

Their three flashlight beams made wavering shadows as they panned around the walls and over stalactites and stalagmites. Droplets of water dripped from the ceiling.

"Look, there's a tunnel. Let's see where it goes," said Miranda as she shined her light on a tall, narrow opening.

"I hope I can squeeze through," said Chris. "I'm not as skinny as you two."

"You can make it," Miranda called to him, already through the opening into another large room. "It gets bigger."

"I made it, but it was a tight fit," Chris told her.

"Wow, look at this!" Laurie said. "It's creepy."

Miranda had to agree as her skin tingled with excitement. The floor tilted downward from the opening they'd come through. Strange formations cast eerie shadows on the glistening walls. The sound of water falling in the distance didn't block out the steady drip, drip, drip near them.

"I think we should go back," Laurie whispered. "Has it been thirty minutes yet?"

Chris checked his watch. "No, just fifteen, and look, this goes on. There's another passage down there."

Miranda started toward it, but her feet slipped out from under her and she slid downward in the wet clay that covered the sloping floor. She stopped herself by digging in her heels and grabbing a stalagmite.

"Are you okay?" Laurie asked in alarm.

"Can you climb back up?" Chris asked.

"It's steeper than it looks, and there isn't much to hold on to, but I'll try," Miranda said. "First let me see what's below me. Hey, it levels out down there. Just a minute, I'm going to look around."

"Miranda, don't..." Laurie began, but Miranda was already sliding.

"Hey this is cool. There's a little pool down here with fish in it. No kidding!" Miranda exclaimed from the level space where she landed.

She stared in awe at the pale, eyeless fish that swam about in the clear water of a long narrow pool. She couldn't tell how deep it was.

"I'm coming down," she heard Chris yell.

"No. We don't know if we can get back up again," Laurie said. "Someone might have to go for help to get Miranda out."

"I'll be careful and look for hand holds along the wall," Chris said. "Shine your light over here,

Laurie, so I can put my flashlight in my pocket and use both hands."

Miranda left the pool and focused the beam of her light on Chris too. He moved with caution, going backward, gripping indentations in the wet surface of the wall.

"Watch your step, Chris. It gets a lot steeper right there."

"Yikes!" Chris screamed as his feet slipped out from under him and he slid on his stomach.

Miranda jumped out of the way.

"Are you okay, Chris?"

"Wet and muddy, is all," he said, getting up and wiping his hands on the back of his jeans. Miranda tried to climb the steep, wet bank, but the slimy clay offered no footing or hand holds.

"Should I go get help?" Laurie asked from above.

"Shhh. Listen!" Miranda said.

She heard voices. It sounded like Josh, Stephanie, and some of the others.

"I don't hear anything," Laurie said.

"It's coming from that way," Chris said, aiming his beam on the opening where a small underground stream trickled from the pond into the darkness.

"This must connect with another passageway!" Miranda said, relieved. "Come on down, Laurie. We'll find the others and go back the way they came."

"Hey, Josh! Wait up." Chris called. "Stay where you are."

His voiced echoed, bouncing back and forth in

the narrow chamber, sending prickles up Miranda's spine. Laurie landed beside her.

"Don't yell, Chris," Laurie said. "It gives me the creeps.

"Their voices were fading away. I didn't want them to go on without us," he said quietly.

"Listen."

The cave was quiet except for the echoes of their whispers.

"Let's go," said Miranda. "We'll follow this little stream until we find them."

They walked in silence, Laurie following Miranda and Chris bringing up the rear.

"Did anyone bring extra batteries? My light's getting dim," Miranda said, stopping.

"Not me," Chris said. Laurie shook her head sadly, her eyes full of fear.

"Let's just use one light at a time so we don't all run out at once," Miranda suggested.

Chris and Laurie turned off their lights and crowded close to Miranda. They walked as quickly and quietly as they could, pausing every few steps to listen. Miranda watched the floor for footprints. The corridor narrowed and the floor rose until they had to get down on their hands and knees to crawl because the ceiling was so close to the floor. The path descended sharply as the corridor widened into a small chamber. Miranda stopped.

"Which way?" she asked, shining her light on three different tunnels leading from the room.

"Look for tracks!" Chris commanded excitedly.

"I bet this is where Josh and the others were when we heard their voices."

He and Laurie turned on their flashlights and they all examined the floor carefully. Most of it was too rocky for any prints to show up.

"Here," said Miranda. "In the mud down this tunnel. Isn't that a footprint?"

They all examined the imprint of a shoe. Farther along, they found larger ones with a different tread, then more of each together.

"Wait a minute," said Laurie. "They're all going away from the room where we found them. I think they're going farther into the cave. If they were headed back, we'd see tracks going both directions."

"You're right," said Miranda uncertainly.

"Should we go back to that room and see if we can see which way they came from?" asked Chris.

"I guess so," Miranda said.

Chris led the way back and they carefully examined each passageway for signs of prints, going a short distance into each one. The rocky floor didn't yield any signs.

"Here are some!" called Laurie with excitement.

Miranda and Chris ran to her and shined their lights on the soft ground a little way up one narrow tunnel.

"Good, let's follow them," Miranda said.

The passageway narrowed and the ceiling got lower as they climbed.

"Stop!" Chris shouted.

"What?" asked Laurie.

"This is the way we came. We're following our own tracks."

Miranda nodded. "Just what I was thinking. Well, let's go back."

They couldn't find any tracks in either of the other tunnels.

"We could pick one and see where it leads," suggested Chris.

"Or we could take the one where we found Josh's tracks and catch up with them. We might meet them coming back. They can tell us which one they came through so we don't wander down the wrong one."

"Okay," said Laurie. "But let's hurry."

Back in the tunnel, Miranda led the way with her dim light while the others saved theirs for later. They stayed as close together as the narrow passageway allowed. Miranda's light became no more than a dull orange circle and then went out completely. Chris pulled his from his pocket, switched it on and handed it to Miranda.

"I'm surprised they haven't come back yet," Laurie whispered several minutes later. "Do you think they're looking for another way out?"

"Listen," Miranda said, stopping again.

"It's the underground stream," said Chris.

"Sounds like a waterfall," Miranda said. "Maybe they'll stop there to look at it. Let's hurry."

They quickened their pace until a scream pierced the air and echoed repeatedly.

Stopping dead in their tracks, they listened, not daring to breath. They heard voices and then sobbing.

Chris called and when his echoes died away, they heard Josh's voice reverberating back to them.

"We're here! Our flashlight died."

"Stay where you are. We're coming," Miranda yelled.

In the yellow glow of Chris's flashlight, Stephanie's face was pale and streaked with tears as she clung to Josh's arm.

"Where are the others?" Laurie asked.

"Didn't you meet them?" Josh asked. "We got lost, so we split up in a small room back there. We were trying to find the way we had come but we all knew we hadn't been in that room before. Some went back the way we came, but we thought this might lead to another way out."

"We came into the same room from a different way," Miranda explained. "We found your tracks so we followed them."

"Then we can go back the way you came in and get out of here!" Josh said excitedly.

"Sorry. We slid down a bank that's impossible to climb. We have to find another way."

"Oh, no. What shall we do?" Stephanie asked between sobs.

"I say we keep going. There's an underground river we've been following. It's got to come out somewhere. We're probably almost there," Josh said.

"Maybe and maybe not," Chris argued. "And even if it does, there might not be any way to follow it. I'm not much in the mood for trying to swim through some tunnel that might not end up anywhere but farther underground."

"Chris has a point," Miranda said, shivering at the thought of getting any wetter than she already was. "I say we go back."

"But we'd never find our way out," Stephanie said. "It's like a maze. There's one place that's very slippery and you could fall a long way off the side, and there's a tiny opening you have to crawl through on your belly. I don't even think Chris could squeeze through."

"Thanks, Steph," Chris growled.

"No offense. I just mean, it was tight for me and you're bigger. I don't want to go back that way."

"Well, we'd better do something," Miranda said, snapping off Chris's light and leaving them in blackness.

"Turn that back on," Stephanie screamed.

"We're going to run out of batteries just standing here. So, until we decide what we're doing, we can stand in the dark."

"Come on," said Josh. "Let's keep going, at least until we see if the way along the river opens up or narrows down. I still think we might be almost to an opening."

Miranda wasn't at all sure. They had been going downhill most of the way. She guessed they were far below the level of the ranch houses by now, but she kept her thoughts to herself. Snapping the light back on she led the way.

"Now which way?" Miranda asked as they entered another small room that split into two tunnels.

The dim yellow light faded and went out. Someone gasped. Laurie turned on her flashlight and panned the walls with its beam.

"That's our last flashlight," Miranda said. "We'd better keep moving."

"Here, you take it, Miranda. I'll follow you."

"The river is on the left. Let's stay as close to it

as we can," Josh suggested.

Miranda took the left opening and they all followed close behind her. Soon they were forced to their hands and knees as the ceiling closed in on them. When they spoke at all, they talked softly to avoid the eerie echoes. Finally they were able to stand again as the floor of the cavern sloped downward. The light was becoming dim. Soon it faded out altogether. Stephanie started crying again.

"Now we'll never get out of here," she sobbed.

"The darkness is so thick and heavy, I feel like it's pressing down on me," Laurie said.

"Me too," Miranda agreed. "Let's go single file, holding on to the one in front of you. We'll go slow and feel our way."

There was no argument. Laurie gripped Miranda's waist.

"Everyone ready?" Miranda asked.

"Yes. I'm bringing up the rear behind Steph and she's holding onto Chris," said Josh.

They all shuffled forward slowly and silently for several minutes.

"Stop! Back up." Miranda shouted.

"What's the matter?" Stephanie hissed.

"Find me a rock or something."

She felt a nudge to her shoulder and reached back to take the small stone that someone handed her. She dropped it and listened as it clunked, tumbled, and rattled until a little splash echoed up to them from far below.

Chapter Five

The silence was finally broken by a sob.

"That could have been you, Miranda. Or all of us," Chris whispered.

"Let's all go back to that last big room. Be careful and stay together," Miranda said. "We're not going any farther in the dark. We'll wait. Someone will find us."

Feeling their way back, they stopped when the walls got so far apart they couldn't touch both of them at once. They sat down, leaned against one wall, and huddled close together. For awhile they talked quietly, trying to cheer each other.

"It won't be long. They probably started looking when we didn't show up when we were supposed to," said Miranda.

"Yeah, or soon after," Josh agreed.

The darkness seemed to shush them, and they fell silent until a long, low rumble broke the stillness.

"That was my stomach growling," Chris said. "I'm starving."

"Me too," Miranda admitted. "Did anyone bring along a lunch?"

"I left mine back at the mouth of the cave. We were going to be back in half an hour," said Josh, "but I brought a canteen. Anyone thirsty?"

Everyone clamored for a drink and passed the canteen back to Josh empty.

"There's a pretty steady drip over here. I had to move to keep it from running down my neck. I'll put the canteen under it," Josh said.

Miranda leaned her head on Chris's shoulder, Laurie rested her's in Miranda's lap. Miranda listened to Stephanie's sobs and the light tap of Josh's hand as he patted her.

"I'm sorry, Steph, but don't worry. We'll be rescued soon." The fear in Josh's voice did little to calm any of them.

Miranda closed her eyes and opened them again. There was no difference in what could be seen. It was totally dark. She closed them again. As she dozed off, she dreamed she was in a sunny meadow, running to meet her beloved horse, Starlight, who was running toward her. She jumped on his back and they galloped together across the broad field. Suddenly, the ground dropped out from under them and they were falling together into darkness

She awakened with a start and opened her eyes. She stifled a scream as she encountered total darkness and remembered where she was. Someone was snoring softly. Laurie's head was heavy in her lap. Miranda's back and legs ached, and she shifted her weight as much as possible without disturbing Laurie. When her heart finally quit pounding she let her head sink against Chris's chest and squeezed her eyes tightly shut. Somehow it was more comforting to be unable to see with your eyes closed than with them open. It seemed like a long time before she drifted off to sleep again.

"Hey! Are you guys all right?" shouted a voice behind a blinding light.

Miranda scrambled to her feet the same time Laurie did.

"Colton, is that you?" Miranda asked, shading her eyes with her hand. "Don't shine that light in my eyes."

"Sorry," Colton said. "I was afraid I was going to have to go back for more rope before I found you."

His light beam focused on the loop of yellow nylon in his hand.

"How did you find us?" asked Miranda. "Is anyone with you?"

She wanted to hug him, for she'd never been so glad to see anyone in her life before. All five of them crowded so close that Colton had to step back.

"I'm the only one skinny enough to get through one very narrow opening. I had to go back twice and have them pass me some more rope. Now all we have to do is follow the line back the way I came, "Colton said. "But first, I have water."

He passed around a canteen, warning everyone to take only a few swallows at a time until they all had an equal share. Josh picked up his own canteen, but there was hardly a mouthful in it. Colton led the way, with Miranda right behind him. His light was getting dim.

"Do you have extra batteries?" Miranda asked.

"Yeah, lots of them. You guys want some?"

He gave some to everyone except Stephanie who had a penlight that needed AAA batteries. Colton lit a candle for her to carry. The extra light was comforting. Before long, Miranda heard the scraping sound of metal against rock.

"We're almost back to that narrow tunnel," Colton informed them. "A couple of men were trying to enlarge it so they could get through. "

"It sounds like it's just around the corner," Stephanie said. "I can't wait to get out of here."

"Sounds are deceiving in here. It's a ways yet. But don't worry; it won't be long," Colton said.

The sound faded away as they trudged uphill, talking softly to each other as they went.

"Looks like they made it," Miranda said, as two flickering lights blinked into view.

"There they are," she heard Mr. Langley say.

"Are they all there? Is everyone okay?" asked a voice that Miranda recognized as Mr. Smythe's.

"Daddy!" cried Stephanie and Laurie at the same time.

When they finally reached the mouth of the cave, Miranda buried her face in her grandmother's coat as her grandma hugged her tight. The sunshine was bright and hurt her eyes for a few minutes, but she was so glad to see it, she didn't think she'd ever be comfortable in the dark again.

"I thought it would be dark by now. It seemed like we were in there a long time.

"It's Friday morning, Miranda," Grandma said. "You were in that cave nearly twenty hours."

Many of the kids' mothers, some of the fathers, and a few other members of the community were there. They all had questions, but Mr. Smythe told them to take their kids home.

"You kids have had enough excitement to last a long time. Get some rest. Don't even try to go back to school today," said Mr. Smythe, who was president of the school board.

Miranda fell asleep on the way home but woke up when Grandma stopped the car in front of the house. The phone was ringing when Miranda walked in the door.

"Miss Hopper got fired!" Laurie said when Miranda answered. "Dad was there when Mr. Smythe told her."

"What happened?"

"Mr. Smythe was furious when he found out that Miss Hopper didn't know where we were. She made the excuse that she had told us to choose a partner and stay together, like it was all our fault."

"Dad said, 'You relied on one kid looking after another in an unexplored cave?' Then she said she told us to be back in half an hour, and we'd have been all right if we had obeyed."

"Didn't any of the kids come back by then?" Miranda asked.

"No. But neither did she. The truth finally came out that she lost track of time and didn't get back until after an hour had passed."

"Wow! I'm surprised she admitted that."

"I don't think she meant to, but she had a hard time explaining why she and Jeb went to town in the bus without us."

"They did? Why?" Miranda asked in surprise.

"Because when she and Jeb finally came out of that chamber, and no one was there, she thought we were trying to play a trick on her by going back to the bus. When they didn't find us there, they drove back to town looking for us. She told him she thought we'd be walking down the road."

"That was stupid! Why would we want to walk back to school when we could be exploring?"

"That's what Mr. Smythe and a lot of the other parents thought," Laurie agreed. "He started yelling at her and told her to get out of his sight. When she started to leave, he told her to go get her things out of the classroom and never come back."

Miranda sat down to a big plate of bacon, eggs, toast, and hash browns. Even though it was past noon, she wanted breakfast, and her Grandma fixed her favorite.

"May I have a bowl of cereal, too?" she asked when she was finished.

"Of course," Grandma said.

After eating, she went out to check on her chickens and rabbits. Grandma and Grandpa had been too worried to think about them and they were hungry and thirsty. She not only fed and watered them, but gave each of them a pat or a hug. Then she asked Grandma if she could go see Starlight.

"No, you've been through quite an ordeal. I want you to get some rest," Grandma said.

"I slept in the cave," Miranda argued. "I'm not really tired."

"Lie down anyway, for an hour at least. You can read, if you want to."

Little Brother crawled onto the bed and lay down against Miranda. She put her arm across his back and closed her eyes. She didn't wake up until Grandpa came in to ask her if she wanted any supper. She ate some soup and went back to bed, sleeping soundly until morning.

Saturday morning's sunrise colored Miranda's room with a rosy glow. She jumped out of bed refreshed and eager to see Starlight. When she arrived at Shady Hills no one else was around, and she was glad to have time alone with her horse. She brushed him quickly and saddled him. She wanted to take him to the river pasture for a quiet ride among the trees as the world was waking up. She remembered her promise to Grandma not to ride far from the stable alone, so she went to the race track instead.

Starlight was eager to run and Miranda let him.

She leaned forward, closed her eyes and enjoyed feeling the wind in her face. When she opened her eyes, she saw Colton standing in the track.

"Glad to see you're okay, kid," he called to her as she stopped beside him.

"Yeah, thanks to you!" Miranda said. "Did the men come and get you when they couldn't get through that narrow place?"

"No, I got there long before they did," Colton said. "I was exercising Starlight when the teacher and her boyfriend came walking up to the bus. When they saw me they asked if I'd seen any of the kids. I told them I hadn't, and they got in the bus and left."

"They didn't say anything? Just left?"

"Oh, yeah, she said, 'They must have started walking, the brats. Just wait until I get my hands on them.'" Colton mimicked the teacher's whiny voice. "I didn't figure anyone started walking or I would have seen them, so I put Starlight back in the paddock, went and got some rope, candles, matches, a flashlight, and extra batteries."

"How did you find the cave?" asked Miranda.

"It wasn't hard to follow the tracks of fourteen people."

"Were all the kids still in the cave when you got there?"

"Yes, but some of them were getting close to finding their way out. I found them in a chamber full of stalagmites and stalactites and they showed me which way they'd gone from there. They went back to the bunkhouse and called their parents while I kept searching."

"So when did Mr. Langley and Mr. Smythe and the rest of the parents get there?"

"I went until I ran out of rope and when I went back to get more, they were all there, organizing a search. They had ropes with them so I took another coil back down to tie on to mine and kept going. Mr. Langley and Mr. Smythe came with me."

"How did you think of using rope? It was a life saver in finding our way back," Miranda said.

"Spelunking is a hobby of mine," Colton said. "If I'd known there was a cave on this place I'd have checked it out before."

"What's spelunking?"

"Exploring caves," Colton said. "The first rule is always leave something to follow, so you can go back the way you came. A person thinks he'll remember where he went, but caves can be disorienting, especially one like this. A light nylon rope is the easiest way to make sure you don't get lost."

"Well, I'm glad you knew what you were doing," Miranda said.

"No problem," Colton said with a grin. "I wish you could come to Denver with us. It won't seem right without you."

"Denver?" Miranda asked, "What are you talking about?"

"The race. Taylor's taking Starlight, Roman Candle, and Fancy to next week's races. We're leaving tomorrow. Didn't he tell you?" Colton asked. "He's all excited about how well Starlight's been running for me. He just can't wait to see him win."

"You think you're going to race Starlight without me being there? Not if I can help it." Miranda said.

Chapter Six

Miranda cried herself to sleep that night, for no matter how she begged, her grandmother was firm. She could not go to Colorado with Mr. Taylor and Starlight.

"You can't afford to miss a week of school, and there is no place for you to stay. Mr. Taylor didn't invite you for good reason. It will just be him, Adam, and Colton. He's not even taking Elliot."

To miss Starlight's race seemed inconceivable to Miranda. She was half-owner, after all, but what good did it do? Yet she knew Grandma's arguments were reasonable. Miranda went to Shady Hills early to see Starlight before he was loaded into the deluxe horse van. The big gooseneck trailer was parked in front of the stable. It had living quarters in front of four padded stalls for horses. The three men would sleep in it while they were away.

"Miranda!" Elliot called to her as she stepped

out of Grandma's car. "Everyone is getting packed and loading the trailer."

"Have they loaded the horses?" Miranda asked.

"No, they haven't even fed them yet. Grandfather said he'd wait until they load them. There will be some hay and oats in the trailer for them."

Miranda brushed Starlight and combed out his silky mane and tail as she talked to him in soft and tearful tones.

"They'd better take good care of you, boy. You watch out and don't let anything bad happen to you. If I were going, I'd stay with you every minute. I'd sleep in your stall. I don't care if you win or lose. I just want you back here safe, again. I never thought Mr. Taylor would take you away from me, even for a week," Miranda said, wiping tears from her eyes.

"Hey, kid," Colton said softly, "I'm sorry you can't come with us. I know how much it means to you. Starlight will miss you. I promise to take good care of him. I'll do everything you taught me and I bet we'll win this race."

"I hope you don't," Miranda said stubbornly, "because if you do, Mr. Taylor will just take him to more and more races, and I don't suppose he'll ever let me go with him."

Colton surprised her by squeezing her shoulders, but he said nothing, letting her know by his silence that he understood.

Holding back tears, Miranda smiled bravely as she led Starlight into the trailer. After watching

Roman Candle and two other horses being loaded, she stepped back to wave good-bye. Adam kept his eyes on the road as he drove the big crewcab pickup with dual rear wheels. It was painted to match the goose neck horse trailer with the Shady Hills logo painted on each side. Mr. Taylor rolled down the passenger side window.

"Don't worry. We'll be back with some trophies!" he shouted as they drove by her.

She couldn't hold back her tears any longer. She dashed to the barn, quickly climbed the ladder, and threw herself upon a pile of hay. She sobbed until she finally fell asleep. When she awoke, she couldn't remember where she was for a few moments. When she went back outdoors, there was a cold breeze coming from the north, and it had started snowing. No one was around. When she knocked at Higgins' door, he was surprised to see her.

"I thought you left when the Wagners came and picked up Elliot," Higgins said. "I figured I was the only one on the place."

"I was in the hay loft. I fell asleep," Miranda explained. "I guess Laurie and Chris aren't coming today. May I use your phone to call Grandma to come get me?"

"Sure, or you can stay and see if you can beat an old man at a game of checkers."

Miranda started to say she just wanted to go home, but changed her mind when she looked at his eager smile. As they played one game after another, they talked about horses. Higgins told her stories of

his youth when he trained some of the best race horses in the country.

"How did you come to work for Mr. Taylor?" Miranda asked.

"We grew up together. I was just a little older and lived on a neighboring farm down in Texas," Higgins began. "Farms and ranches and all the little towns were far apart, so there weren't many other kids to play with. Cash's parents didn't think much of me because I came from a poor family of dirt farmers. They had money. But Cash and I have always been friends. I spent a lot of time around the Taylors' horses. I had a way with them. When Cash finally got fed up with his parents and moved to Montana, he asked me to come work for him. I was in Virginia by then, making good money training race horses."

"Did Mr. Taylor offer you more money?"

"No, he said I'd have to work for room and board only, until he got started. It took every cent he had to buy this ranch. He was able to bring a few mares with him from Texas. When he found Cadillac's Last Knight, he mortgaged everything to buy him. But it was a good move."

"Had Knight already won a lot of races?"

"No, he was not quite two years old and wild as a March hare!" Higgins exclaimed. "It was my job to train him for the track."

"Wow, I'm surprised Mr. Taylor would spend that much money on a horse that hadn't been proven," Miranda said.

"He had a feeling about him. Cash has an uncanny sense when it comes to horses. He had the same feeling about your Starlight. And he was right. I used to think Knight was the fastest horse that ever lived, but Starlight is faster."

When Miranda walked into the sixth grade classroom Monday morning, she saw Preston Langley,

Laurie's father standing near the door. Fear shot through her. A few months before, the Langleys had talked about moving. Maybe he had come to take her out of school. She looked frantically around the classroom before she saw her best friend sitting calmly at her desk reading a book.

"Laurie," Miranda whispered, slipping into the desk in front of her, "what is you dad doing here?"

"He's the new teacher," Laurie answered with a broad smile. "Mr. Smythe called an emergency meeting of the school board Friday night. He got dad hired to take Miss Hopper's place. Now dad can stay home instead of being out on the road most of the time."

Miranda looked into her best friend's sparkling eyes and knew that Laurie felt as relieved and happy as she did. Laurie had feared that her parents would move away because of the discrimination against them in the community.

The Langleys had moved here expecting Mr. Langley to teach math in the high school, but the school board had withdrawn the job offer after they saw him. It was a great disappointment to the Langleys, especially since it was clear that the loss of the job was all because of the color of his skin. He'd stayed in the town anyway, but it was hard for Laurie's blonde, blue-eyed, vivacious mother to endure the snubs from the community. The tension between the Smythes and the Langleys eased after Mr. Langley saved Mr. Smythe's son from a deadly fire.

When the bell rang and the classroom became quiet, Mr. Langley took charge. He was gentle and quiet, but allowed no nonsense. When he asked how the students were coming on their research papers, not one of them had even started.

"Well, get started. I will be checking on your progress. You don't have much time left. By next Monday morning, I want to see note cards with information from at least four different sources," he told them. "Oh, by the way, I see Miss Potter asked for twenty pages. I'm shortening that to seven plus a title page and a bibliography."

He asked each student what subject they were going to research and where they were going to find the information. When Miranda asked if she could research the history of horse racing, he said, "Sure."

"May I include a personal interview as one of my sources? I know a race horse trainer."

He readily agreed and suggested it was a good idea for anyone who wanted to include a personal interview as one of their sources.

The weather turned cold, windy, and snowy during the week that Starlight was gone. Miranda worried about her horse, but worked hard on her chores and her school assignments and went to bed exhausted so she wouldn't have time to think about him. She helped her grandparents with the extra feeding that the snow and cold demanded. Little Brother followed her everywhere, and stood protectively outside the chicken house door when she went inside to put extra straw in the nests and the rabbit hutches.

As she finished supper Friday evening, the phone rang.

"It's for you, Miranda," Grandpa said.

"Hi, Miranda, we're home and we won. You should have seen Starlight. He was so far ahead of the pack, people couldn't quit talking about him!" Colton said.

Miranda begged to go immediately to Shady Hills, but her grandparents said Saturday morning would be soon enough.

By the time Grandpa was ready to go after another load of hay from the Miller ranch, Miranda was frantic with impatience. She called both Laurie and Chris to make sure they would be ready. Laurie ran out the front door as Grandpa stopped in front of the Langley home. Chris was still inside the store, and Miranda ran in to get him. He wasn't quite ready.

"Hurry up, Chris. I've got to see Starlight."

"Is he leaving or something?" Chris asked with irritating sarcasm. "I don't think five minutes is going to make much difference."

When they finally arrived, Miranda dashed to Starlight's stall. He whinnied when he saw her. She hugged him as he pressed his head against her chest. She offered him carrots and apple slices which he ate greedily. It was such a relief to be with her horse again, that Miranda closed her eyes and fervently prayed that they would never part again.

"Hi," Colton called from the doorway, interrupting her reverie. "Mr. Taylor told me to keep exercising and riding him. He's going to California in December for an even bigger race against some of the fastest horses in the Western United States."

Miranda's heart sank. It would never end. Mr. Taylor would take her horse all over the world, leaving her behind.

When Miranda got home that evening, Grandma told her to call her mother.

"Miranda, I'm asking a big favor of you. I know you hate to be away from your horse, even for a little while, but, I really want to spend Christmas with you this year," Mom said over the phone. "I can't get away to come there, so I want you to come here. I'll get an airline ticket for you, if you will just say yes."

"I don't know. I'll have to ask Grandma," Miranda said, not wanting to say no, yet not really wanting to go.

"Grandma said it would be fine," Mom said. "I already asked her."

"Well, then, I guess so," Miranda said, then asked, "Do I have to decide tonight?"

"I need to know soon, so I can get the ticket while it is still affordable."

"I'll let you know for sure by tomorrow night."

At Shady Hills the next day, Miranda asked Colton, "What is the date of the race in California and where is it?"

"I don't know. You'll have to ask Mr. Taylor."

"December twenty-eighth, twenty-ninth and thirtieth," Mr. Taylor said, "at Los Alamitos race track."

"Is that anywhere near Los Angeles?" Miranda asked.

"Why yes, that's where it is."

Miranda had never flown before. A knot of fear and excitement welled up inside her as she hugged her grandparents good-bye and boarded the small airplane at Gallatin Field on the twenty-second of December. It was snowing pretty hard and very cold. Flying would be scary until they got above the clouds. *It'll be fun*, she told herself, as she tried to calm the butterflies in her stomach. She concentrated on the fact that she was going to get to see all of Starlight's races — Mom had promised. Christmas away from her grandparents would feel strange. It would be nice to spend the holiday with her mother if she didn't have to share her with Margot and little Kort, two children she didn't even know; and worst of all, with Adam.

Chapter Seven

When Miranda arrived at LAX, the airport in Los Angeles, it was a balmy seventy, and she carried her warm parka over her arm. She wished she wasn't wearing her heavy sweater. People surged around her, and Miranda scanned the crowd for a familiar face. She had waited on the plane until an attendant could escort her and officially hand her over to her mother.

"There she is!" Miranda said, pointing. "Mom!"

The attendant had to look up into the blue eyes of Carey Stevens as she greeted her cheerfully.

"I must see your I.D., Mrs. Stevens," the attendant said before releasing Miranda's hand.

The airline was responsible for a minor traveling unattended, and they wouldn't even take Miranda's word that this tall, slender young woman was her mother.

"Oh, Mandy, I'm so glad to see you!" her mother exclaimed, hugging her closely. "Come on. Adam and

Margot are waiting at the baggage claim. As soon as we get your luggage, we'll go eat and maybe do some shopping before we go home."

Miranda's heart sank. She'd hoped that she would have her mother to herself for at least this one afternoon. Soon she found herself in the back seat of a car next to a strangely quiet little girl. Adam drove and Mom sat next to him, pointing out sights and giving Adam directions. Miranda wished she was back at Shady Hills with Starlight.

She stole sideways glances at the girl next to her. Margot was about the same size as Elliot. She had smoky blonde hair and a little turned up nose on her thin face. A hint of freckles peppered her nose and cheeks. Margot kept her head forward and her eyes on the floor. She didn't look as if she enjoyed being part of this troupe any more than Miranda did. Miranda sighed and looked out the window. There were cars and tall buildings everywhere.

"Where would you two girls like to eat?" Mom asked, twisting around in her seat to look at them.

Margot didn't move or raise her eyes. She said nothing. Miranda began to wonder if there was something wrong with her. If she was mentally retarded or something, why hadn't Mom told her?

"Miranda, where do you want to eat?" her mother repeated.

"I'm not really hungry," Miranda said.

Mom and Adam took them to a restaurant near the ocean. One side of the room was lined with pin ball machines and video games. On the wall near their

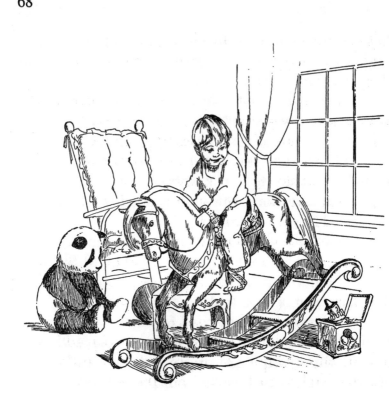

table was a big screen TV that played old cartoons. Miranda sat and stared out the window at the waves breaking on the narrow beach and the sea gulls circling and squawking; landing and fighting over some morsel, then flying up again. At first Adam and Mom tried to engage the girls in conversation. When that failed, they talked about people and things of which Miranda had no knowledge or interest.

"Well, look at the time!" Mom exclaimed at last. "I've got to be back to look after Kort in an hour. It'll take that long to drive home."

Kort, the son of a rich fashion model who employed Carey as a nanny, was a chubby, talkative two and a half year old. His dark grey eyes sparkled as he darted about, laughing and chattering.

"Kortie's got a horsie. Manda come see?" he asked, reaching for Miranda's hand.

Miranda found him irresistible and joined him in play when he led her to his room. The "horsie" was a tall rocking horse. There was a little foot stool beside it to help him climb on. He rocked so hard and fast, she feared he would fall off, but then he rolled off in one easy motion, landing on his feet and running to another toy across the room which he demanded that, "Manda come see."

Miranda didn't know where Margot had gone, nor did she care. Adam and Mom were in the den, or library or whatever it was called, picking out Christmas music. Miranda only wanted to stay out of their way until Adam left. It shouldn't be hard in the huge house. The living room was as big as the kitchen, dining and living room of her grandparents' farm house, all put together. It was full of furniture that looked as if it had never been sat upon. Big paintings hung on the walls, and marble and bronze statues stood near an enormous fire place. The floor was covered with a fluffy white carpet. In a smaller room next to it was a grand piano. Big glass doors led to a patio filled with a variety of flowering plants, bird feeders and a bird bath, and other ornamental statues.

Miranda didn't have time to explore all of the house before her mother announced that it was bed time and led her up a winding staircase with a brightly polished banister.

"You'll sleep in here with Margot. Maybe the two of you can get acquainted," her Mom suggested.

The room was large and furnished with identical twin beds. Margot was sitting on one with her back to the door. She didn't turn when Mom and Miranda came in.

"Margot, honey," Mom said softly. "Do you need anything before you go to bed?"

There was no reply other than a slight head shake.

"Well, I'll be in the room across the hall, Miranda. If either of you need anything, come and get me," Mom said, patting Miranda's hair. "I'll come tuck you in before I go to bed."

Miranda put on her flannel pajamas, dropping her jeans and sweat shirt on the floor beside the bed. She soon decided it was far too hot in this room to have the fluffy comforter pulled up. She kicked it off, then she threw off her pajama top. Margot was still sitting on the edge of the bed when Miranda turned off the lamp that stood on the bedside table. Lying still, she heard the slightest movement and saw the silhouette of the the little girl disappear under the covers.

"Good night, Margot," Miranda said.

There was no answer.

Miranda wakened sometime in the middle of the night. She heard sobs coming from the other bed and guessed that Margot had been crying for some time.

"Margot?" she said.

The crying immediately stopped.

"What's the matter, Margot?" Miranda asked softly, "Do you want me to go get Mom?"

"Leave me alone!" came the angry reply from the other bed.

Well at least she can talk, Miranda thought. She lay awake for a long time listening. There was no sound from the other bed except for an occasional sniffle, but Miranda was sure Margot was awake.

When Miranda got up the next morning, she dressed quickly in the jeans that had been picked up from the floor and draped on the back of the chair. She pulled on a light T-shirt with a picture of running horses across the front of it. She could see just the top of Margot's head above the covers. The girl was snoring softly. Miranda found her mother and Adam in the breakfast nook, having coffee and discussing wedding plans. Didn't the guy ever leave?

"Well, good morning!" her mother called to her. "Did you sleep well?"

"I slept okay," she answered, glaring at Adam as she sat down.

"Would you like some hot chocolate?" Mom asked.

Miranda nodded. "Yes, please." Looking at Adam, she said, "You must have gotten up early to get here so soon."

"There are plenty of guest rooms in this big house," he said. "I didn't have to go anywhere."

Great, Miranda thought, *I'll never get to spend a minute alone with Mom.*

"I hear Kort," Mom said as she put a cup of steaming chocolate milk in front of Miranda. "Excuse me while I go get him."

"I'll get him," Miranda offered, jumping up. She didn't want to be left alone with Adam.

When she came back with little Kort in her arms, his tousled brown head resting on her shoulder, Mom looked up with a smile.

"He sure likes you! How would you like to spend the day helping me look after Kort? Adam is going to take Margot out and spend the day with her. I thought we might take Kort to the zoo or the aquarium and then to the Play Place for lunch."

"Really?" Miranda asked, "I'd love that!"

"Mom, do you really love Adam?" Miranda asked suddenly as they drove back home, Kort asleep in his car seat.

They'd had a wonderful time, laughing with little Kort as he ran excitedly from one new discovery to another. Miranda saw a side of her mother she hadn't seen before. All her attention was on Kort and Miranda, making sure that they were both having a good time. Mom obviously loved the little tyke and Miranda felt a strong surge of love for her mother. It made her long for a kinship they had never enjoyed.

"Why, of course," her mother answered. "Why else would I marry him?"

Miranda shrugged and looked away. Mom

pulled the car into a parking lot and stopped.

"You don't like him much, do you?" her mother asked, as she gently reached for Miranda's chin and turned her face toward her. "Why not?"

"He doesn't like me, and I don't think he even likes his own daughter."

"Of course he does," Mom answered. "He hasn't had much chance to get to know her, but how could he not love her?"

Remembering how strangely sullen and distant the little girl was, Miranda didn't think it would be too hard.

"What do you like about him?" Miranda asked.

"Well, he's drop dead handsome," her mother said with a laugh. "He's sweet, generous, and smart."

"Hmmff!" Miranda snorted. "We must be talking about two different guys."

"Mandy, it's been hard for me to be alone all these years since your father left. My heart was broken and I never thought I'd be able to fall in love again. I think I finally have, so I hope you'll try to see the good in him, for my sake."

Miranda looked into her mother's eyes and was surprised to see them filled with tears. She wanted to say that it hadn't seemed to her that her mother had been alone. She'd dated one guy after another until there was no keeping track of them all. But she couldn't say anything hurtful when her mother already looked so sad.

"I guess I can try," Miranda said.

"And Margot. Maybe you can befriend her.

She's very lonely. It will be hard for her to be without her mother on Christmas. I take it they were very close, and it's only been a few months since she died."

Once again, Miranda heard Margot sobbing, long after they had gone to bed.

"Margot?" she whispered, "would it help to talk about it?"

The sobbing immediately stopped.

"Margot?" Miranda asked again.

There was no answer. Miranda waited, wondering what she could say to break through the wall of silence, but she fell asleep before any ideas came.

Chapter Eight

On Christmas morning, Miranda woke up missing her grandparents, her friends, and most of all, her horse. She asked her mother's permission to call Montana. She talked to both Grandma and Grandpa who missed her too. They told her that Uncle Corey, Aunt Jolene, and eighteen month old Cody Kyle were coming for a late dinner. Miranda wished she was there to see them. She loved playing with her baby cousin. She called Laurie.

"Colton has been working with Starlight everyday. That horse just loves to run," Laurie told her. "But I think he misses you," she added quickly. "Colton said they're going to load up Starlight, Roman Candle, and Fancy tomorrow morning and head for California."

Kort was up, dancing around the Christmas tree, running from one brightly wrapped present to another, when Miranda got off the phone.

"Are you going to let him open them?" Miranda

asked Mom.

"Not yet. His mother's still sleeping. She got in late last night from Milan. I'm sure she wants to watch him open the gifts she brought for him," Mom said. "Besides, Margot hasn't come out of her room yet. Let's wait until we're all together."

It was nearly noon when Lorna Schoffler, a tall, willowy model with striking auburn hair, came into the living room. Miranda was told to go get Margot. Margot refused to come.

"Please, Margot," Miranda pleaded, "everyone is waiting for you. Kort has had to wait so long already."

"Open your presents without me. I don't want any."

"I don't think it would hurt you to watch Kort have some fun," Miranda said, suddenly angry. "Maybe you should quit feeling sorry for yourself and think about someone else for a change."

Margot glared at her until she had to turn away to blink back tears.

"Fine," she said, brushing past Miranda and stomping toward the living room.

Kort was sitting in the midst of a pile of torn wrapping paper, pulling a toy train engine from a box. They hadn't waited. Miranda glanced at Margot who only stared at the floor.

Miranda begged her mother to take her to Los Alamitos race track as early as possible on the twenty-eighth but her mother looked at her apologetically.

"I'm sorry, Mandy. Kort is sick this morning. Too much Christmas candy, I suppose. I'm going to have to stay here with him. Adam will take you and Margot after he gets up and has some breakfast."

Adam took his sweet time. Margot said she didn't want to go, and Adam got angry and yelled at her. He said much the same thing that Miranda had said to her on Christmas morning, only he came right out and called her a selfish little whiner. Miranda wished she could take back her own hasty words; she certainly didn't agree with Adam. Nor did Mom.

"Adam, I don't think you mean that!" Mom exclaimed, putting a protective arm around Margot. "You're welcome to stay with me and Kort, if you want to, honey. But with him being sick as he is, I think you might find the race track more exciting."

Miranda saw the angry look that Adam flashed toward her mother. Mom didn't, for she was giving all her attention to Adam's daughter. In the end, Margot decided to go to the track, but sat sullenly silent for the whole trip.

It took awhile to find Mr. Taylor. There were a million horse trailers in the stable area, or so it seemed to Miranda. People were leading horses in all directions. At last, Miranda spotted the horse van with the Shady Hills logo on it. Mr. Taylor was coming out of the little bedroom compartment in the front of it.

"Mr. Taylor!" Miranda shouted, breaking into a run. She never dreamed she'd be so happy to see the crotchety old man. She ran to him and hugged him hard.

"Glad you're here, Miranda," Mr. Taylor said.

He sounded as if he really meant it and smiled as he took her hand and led her to the stall where Starlight waited. Colton was rummaging through a big wooden box that was marked Shady Hills Horse Ranch. Starlight nickered when he saw her and began raking the inside of his stall door with his hoof. She ran to him, cradled his face between her hands, and kissed him on the nose. He rubbed his upper lip on her neck as if he were kissing her back.

Elliot stood in line to greet Miranda.

"I was waiting for you to come," he said with a smile, then whispered, "Is that Adam's daughter?"

Miranda had forgotten all about Margot and turned to see her standing, wide eyed, next to her father. She was actually very pretty, Miranda suddenly realized. She wondered what she would look like if she would smile.

"Elliot, this is Margot Barber," she said. "Margot, this is Elliot. His grandfather owns Shady Hills."

"Hi, Margot," Elliot said with a big smile. "Do you want me to show you the other horses we brought?"

Margot looked uncertainly at Adam. He nodded and she followed Elliot. The two were the same height and Elliot sounded like a little tour guide as, in his enchanting British accent, he told the names and history of every horse they passed.

When they disappeared around a corner, Miranda turned back to Starlight. When Colton said it was time to put Starlight on the exercise wheel, Miranda insisted on longeing him instead. After Starlight had been running in circles around Miranda, first one way and then the other, for several minutes, Miranda glanced up to see a crowd of people watching them. Mr. Taylor must have noticed, too.

"That's enough for now, Miranda," he said. "Bring him in."

Miranda stayed until just before post time when Colton was on Starlight's back, being led onto the track to parade before the grandstand. Then she went with Mr. Taylor, Adam, Margot, and Elliot to the box that Mr. Taylor had reserved just above the finish line. How Miranda envied Colton. She wanted to be in his place more than anything! Knowing that would probably never happen, she used binoculars to watch Starlight's every move. Every muscle in her body was tense as she waited for the race to begin.

She would be helping put Starlight in the starting gate if Mr. Taylor would have let her, but he said it was no place for a little girl. He would not be responsible for having her trampled, he told her. But it was no problem. Starlight walked into the gate as calmly as he walked into his stall when she fed him each day. He didn't seem the least bit nervous. She could see Colton's lips moving as he patted the stallion on the neck. She knew he was talking in a soft soothing voice, just as she did whenever she rode him. Jealous as she was of him for being the one to ride, she couldn't help feeling grateful that he treated Starlight exactly as she had shown him.

Suddenly they were off. Starlight surged ahead of the pack on his first leap out of the gate and steadily widened his lead.

"Your rider is going to use him up and have nothing left for the finish," said a man to Mr. Taylor. "Look at number fourteen. That's my horse. See how my rider is saving him? He'll put on a burst of speed in the back stretch while your horse is slowing down."

Miranda smiled to herself. She knew what Colton knew. Trying to slow Starlight down at any point in the race would have caused a fight between horse and rider. Starlight was having fun. He had plenty left to give. As she watched, the black stallion did slow down and seemed to be looking back for the other horses.

"Come on you guys," he seemed to be saying. "Where is everyone?"

As a tall bay mare came up on the inside, Starlight actually turned his head and touched her on the nose. "That's more like it," Miranda could almost hear Starlight say. "Let's race, shall we?"

The bay mare surged ahead as her rider leaned forward and began using the crop. Starlight lengthened his stride and stayed even with her. Colton still sat relaxed in the saddle. As they rounded the back stretch, several other horses crowded into a pack near the two leaders. Miranda watched as Colton slowly leaned farther over Starlight's withers. She knew he was saying, "Okay, boy. You can go now."

Starlight burst forward, pulling away from the mare and the rest of the pack as if they were standing still. By the time he reached the finish line he was two lengths ahead of a gray gelding that edged out the mare to come in second.

Miranda ran to the winner's circle and threw her arms around her horse's neck. Colton stood proudly beside him, his face stretched with the wide grin that Miranda had become so used to seeing.

"What an outstanding performance by Sir Jet Propelled Cadillac, ridden by Colton Spencer, owned by Cassius Taylor of Shady Hills Ranch in Montana," the announcer said. "Is Mr. Taylor here to accept the winner's wreath?"

"He's coming," Miranda said, stepping up to the man with the microphone. "I'm Starlight's other owner. I own a half share."

"Starlight?"

"That's what we call him. That's what everyone in Montana knows him by," she explained as she fondly stroked Starlight's cheek. "Sir Jet Propelled Cadillac is just his registered name."

"All right, then, ladies and gentlemen, Starlight, owned by Cassius Taylor and...," the announcer held the microphone in front of Miranda.

"Miranda Stevens," she said.

"and Miranda Stevens is our winner."

Mr. Taylor was frowning as he walked into the winner's circle and reached for the big circle of flowers that was being held out to him. He placed it around Starlight's neck.

"Do you have anything to say about the performance of this animal, Starlight, Mr. Taylor?" asked the announcer. "Is Miranda actually part owner?"

"She would have to make sure the world knows her horse by the name she gave him," Mr. Taylor said. "Yes. She's half owner and his trainer, as well."

Miranda looked at Mr. Taylor in surprise. She had expected to be scolded, but instead he was smiling at her. He took her by the hand as she led Starlight back to the stables.

Miranda was almost asleep when a faint whispering sound roused her from her reverie. She listened a moment before she decided it was her imagination. She went back to thinking of the three days of racing in which Starlight had easily won every race. Roman Candle had won two. Fancy had come in second to a coal black mare who had no white on her anywhere. Miranda suggested that Mr. Taylor buy her, but he hadn't seemed interested. Miranda was dozing off when she heard it again. She opened her eyes and listened.

"Miranda, are you awake?" Margot was whispering so softly that Miranda could barely hear her.

"Yes, what is it, Margot?" Miranda asked as she got out of bed and tiptoed across the room. "May I sit on your bed?"

"Yes," came the soft voice.

"Can't you sleep?" Miranda asked as she sat next to Margot and reached for her hand.

"Miranda, I want to go with you when you go home tomorrow."

"You do?" Miranda could hardly believe her ears. "I thought you didn't like me much."

"I do. I thought you didn't like me," Margot said softly. "I don't like living here. I hate school. Would you hate it if I came to Montana?"

"No, of course not. Is your dad moving back with you, or would you like to live with me?"

"With you, if I could," she whispered, squeezing Miranda's hand.

Chapter Nine

The girls sat side by side on the big airplane. It hadn't been easy to get Margot on the same flight as Miranda, but someone had canceled at the last minute. Miranda was amazed they had pulled it off. Adam hadn't seemed to care, and though a little hurt that Margot didn't want to stay, Mom thought the change might be what the sad child needed. Grandma and Grandpa agreed after Miranda assured them that she didn't mind sharing her room.

As Margot sat in silence, Miranda began to have second thoughts. She'd always had her room to herself. But when Grandma had pointed that out to her, she had brushed it off as unimportant.

"I know how to share," she had retorted. "If I don't, it's probably time I learned."

"I just want you to be sure. Once she's here, it will be too late to change your mind."

These words echoed in Miranda's mind now.

She wondered what it would really be like. She hardly knew Margot and had never particularly liked her. But she had felt sorry for her at the time. Or maybe it was that she'd been happy to learn that the little girl actually liked her well enough to want to be with her. But now it occurred to Miranda that Margot might not like her at all, but decided she was the better of two evils. She wanted to get out of the city, the big school, away from a teacher she didn't like, and Miranda was her ticket.

The sun was shining brightly and ice crystals could be seen in the air as they landed at Gallatin Field near Belgrade, Montana. Grandma and Grandpa were waiting to greet them. After hugging Miranda, Grandma knelt in front of Margot and opened her arms.

"Hi, Margot, I'm Kathy Greene, but I much prefer to be called Grandma, if you can be comfortable with that."

Miranda stared over Grandpa's arm as he enveloped her in a hug. She saw Margot's face relax with relief as she plunged into Grandma's embrace. Margot clung tightly to Grandma's hand as they left the warm terminal for the car. She stopped as the crisp cold air hit her face.

"Chilly, isn't it?" Grandpa asked, from behind her.

"It's so cold it feels like my nose is freezing shut!" Margot exclaimed, "but it looks so warm."

"That's Montana," Miranda said with a laugh. "Don't worry, you'll get used to it."

Miranda stopped in the doorway of her bedroom. Her bed was gone and in its place was a twin sized bed with another one crowded in against the opposite wall. There was hardly room to walk between the foot of her bed and her chest of drawers. Her desk had been moved into the living room.

"Where's my bed and where did you get these?" Miranda asked her grandmother.

"I had them stored in the attic," Grandma explained, placing her hand on Miranda's shoulder, "and that's where your double bed is now. These beds belonged to your Mom and Uncle Corey when they shared this room when they were little. That one was Corey's bed. The one you'll sleep in used to be your mother's. They can be stacked as bunk beds, if you'd prefer, but I'm afraid the ladder that goes with it got broken and thrown out long ago."

"It sure makes it crowded. I think it would be better if they were stacked," Miranda said.

"What do you think, Margot?" Grandma asked.

"It's okay with me if I can have the bottom. I don't like sleeping up high."

"You want the top bunk, Miranda?"

"No. I don't mind heights, but Little Brother couldn't get up there. He's used to sleeping with me."

"Well, let's try them as they are for now. I think you'll find you have plenty of room."

Miranda was not so sure of it. She was beginning to wish she'd left Margot in California.

When Miranda heard Margot sniffling later that night, she turned over and pulled the covers over her ear. *I hope I'm not going to have to listen to that every night. I don't suppose anything can make this girl happy. She's selfish...* Miranda thought as she reached over to put her arm around Little Brother. He wasn't there. She opened her eyes and sat up, feeling on both sides of the bed and at the foot. Little Brother, now almost as big as a small pony should not be hard to find.

She turned on the lamp beside her bed. There was the black dog, front paws on Margot's bed, licking her face. She saw Margot's hand come out from under the blankets and pat Little Brother's head. The blankets lifted and Little Brother climbed in under them.

Traitor, thought Miranda as she turned off the light again.

Miranda put the finishing touches on her research paper at school the next day. She had worked hard on it before Christmas vacation and only needed to type out the bibliography before turning it in. It had been fun, once she got started and she learned a lot more about horse racing than she'd ever known before. Higgins helped, not only by relating his experiences, but by asking questions that led Miranda to more research in the library.

When Mr. Langley handed the term papers back a week later, Miranda got an almost perfect score with a few points taken off for punctuation, but extra points given for content. "You made the subject exciting to read; informative and intriguing," Mr. Langley had written on her paper.

School was actually fun now. The new teacher made each class as interesting as possible. Math was hard for Miranda and she would have given up if Mr. Langley hadn't always seemed happy to explain until she understood the concept. Sometimes that took a long time. Everyone in the class said they liked the new teacher. Except for Bill. Soon after Mr. Langley came to teach, Bill quit coming to school.

"Bill's been absent for several days now," Laurie said as they rode to Shady Hills with Chris and his mother. "Maybe we should call and find out what's wrong with him."

"Probably a bad case of the flu. You miss him, don't you Laurie? I think you have a crush on him," Miranda teased.

"I do not!" Laurie declared, blushing. "I just thought it would be nice if everyone sent get well cards or something."

"He's not sick," Chris told them. "His mother decided to home school him."

"Why?" asked Laurie in alarm.

"Well, uh," Chris stammered. "No offense but I think..."

"You don't know the reason," Chris's mother interrupted. "Maybe she just wanted to supervise his education. A lot of parents are doing that you know."

Miranda watched Laurie slump back into the seat and look down at her folded hands as tears flooded her eyes.

The winter went by quickly with little communication between Miranda and Margot. Miranda was too busy with school, friends, chores, and Starlight to pay much attention to the quiet child who now shared her home. Margot seemed happy at school, whenever Miranda saw her in the halls. She was often with Elliot and sometimes even rode his bus home so she could play with him until one of the parents came to take them home.

"Little Brother is sleeping with me, tonight," Miranda informed Margot one night as they were getting ready for bed. "He's my dog and always slept with me before you came. Get your own dog if you want one to sleep with."

"Grandpa said Little Brother belongs to all of us," Margot replied.

"Look. You wanted to come to Montana. But I didn't know you were going to take over everything I have, including my grandparents!" Miranda shouted.

"You don't want me here," Margot said quietly, looking down.

Miranda saw a tear glistening on her cheek.

"I didn't say that. I just said..." Miranda began. *This isn't your home,* is what she'd almost said. But when she thought how mean that would sound she stopped herself. What would it be like to have no home at all? No mother, a dad who didn't want her — a dad like Adam!

"I'm sorry, Margot," Miranda began again. "It's not that I don't want you. I just wish I knew you better. You never talk to me and I can't even imagine what it feels like, well you know — not to be able to live with your mother anymore. You loved her a lot didn't you?"

"I miss my mom so much," Margot said, tears streaming down her face. "Your grandparents are very nice to me. Sometimes they make me almost forget..."

"Don't be afraid to tell me how you feel," Miranda said. "Are you sorry you came here?"

"Only at night when I get to thinking you wish I wasn't here. I know you don't like sharing your room with me. I like school. The teacher's nice and all the kids are good to me. Elliot is my best friend. He knows what it's like to..." Margot stopped and wiped her eyes. "His mother died too, you know."

"I know. I'm so sorry. It must be awful! I don't live with my mom, but I know she loves me, and I could go live with her if I wanted."

"Do you want me to leave?" Margot asked, looking straight into Miranda's eyes. "My dad's moving back, and he said he'd get an apartment if I want to live with him."

"No!" Miranda exclaimed, adding more softly, "No. I really don't. I just want you to talk to me once in awhile."

"Like you talk to me!" Margot exclaimed. "Sometimes I want to talk to you so bad, but you're already sleeping. You just come in and glare at me and then go to bed."

Miranda started to deny this accusation, but when she thought about it she realized she hadn't made it easy for Margot to talk to her.

"I'm sorry. It hasn't been easy for me, either. I

don't like sharing my room, but I'm getting used to it, and I want you to stay. I want to know more about you and how you're feeling. I'd like to be able to tell you how my day went sometimes."

When the lights were turned out, Margot whispered, "Miranda, if we're going to talk, do you think I could lie in your bed? I don't like talking loud."

"I was just thinking the same thing. Come here."

"I used to snuggle with Mama like this when I got scared at night," Margot confided as she pulled Miranda's arm across her shoulder.

"Your mama must have been very loving, like Elliot's mum," Miranda said.

"Oh yes! Elliot and I talk about our mothers a lot. They were both fun and kind and..." Margot's voice trailed off and she sniffled.

"Elliot's dad wasn't so great. He left as soon as he found out his wife had cancer," Miranda said.

"My dad left before I was born. He came back and lived with my mom for about two months after he got out of the navy. I was a baby then. I think that's why he left. He visited twice after I was old enough to remember, but only for an hour or two. Then I never saw him again until after Mama died."

"What do you think of him, now?" Miranda asked, anger against Adam Barber flaring again inside her.

"I think he wishes he didn't have me," Margot said in a whisper. "I think the only reason he asked me to live with him is because your mom thinks he should. I suppose I'll have to live with him after he marries your mother."

The girls talked long into the night and Margot fell asleep next to Miranda and stayed there until morning.

"Grandma," Miranda said at breakfast the next morning. "we'd like to have my old bed back and put Mom's and Corey's back in the attic."

"That can be arranged if it's something you both want," Grandma said, looking at Margot.

Miranda watched the corners of Margot's mouth turn up. The smile Miranda had been waiting for brightened Margot's eyes as she nodded.

On a cold windy day in late February, Miranda and Margot rode the bus home after school. It was Grandpa's birthday and Grandma was making all his favorite foods for supper. If the girls helped with the chores, they'd get done early to celebrate. Miranda hurried to the milk barn where Grandpa was rationing grain for the first six cows that would come in for milking. Miranda opened the door and let them in.

"Miranda, there's a heifer in the calving pen. I think she's getting close," Grandpa said a half hour later. "Would you go check on her? Don't go in the pen, just climb up on the fence and see how she's doing."

Miranda hurried outside and climbed the rail fence next to the barn. The heifer was standing in one corner, her back hunched, straining. As Miranda watched, the head appeared and very quickly a wet little black and white body slipped to the ground. The heifer turned toward her baby, but didn't start licking it as she'd seen other cows do. Instead, the mother butted it with her head. She seemed to have gone crazy, acting like she wanted to kill the calf.

"Grandpa, come quick! She just had it, and now she's trying to kill it!" Miranda shouted as she rushed into the barn.

Grandpa came running, jumped over the fence, and dashed to pick up the helpless calf as the cow turned away from it.

"Watch out!" Miranda screamed.

But it was too late. Before Grandpa could make it to the fence, the young cow charged at him, hit him in the middle of the back, and slammed him against the fence. Grandpa fell to the ground, dropping the calf. Neither of them moved. The cow was backing up, head down, getting ready to charge again.

Chapter Ten

"No!" Miranda yelled, jumping into the corral. She ran between Grandpa and the cow toward the gate. She climbed over just before the enraged beast rammed it with her head. The cow staggered backward. Miranda unfastened the latch and swung the gate open as the cow came charging after her again. When the cow rushed through the gate, Miranda slammed it shut and raced back to her grandfather.

"Grandpa, please don't be dead!" she shouted, sobbing. "Grandpa?"

Grandpa groaned and coughed. His face was white, but he reached out his hand to touch her face.

"I'm okay, Mandy. I had the wind knocked out of me. Where's the cow?"

"Out the gate. I shut it."

"Bless you," he whispered. "My back and chest hurt something awful. Run and tell Grandma to call an ambulance. Then bring me a blanket."

Miranda ran, but it seemed like slow motion. She couldn't get there fast enough. Everything seemed to be happening a long way off, like in a dream. She was trying to make her legs work, but it felt like a nightmare she had once where it took every ounce of strength to move them. She had never been so scared in her life. She couldn't breathe.

Margot and Grandma dashed after her to the small corral where Grandpa lay softly moaning. Miranda tucked blankets around her grandfather, then lay with her head on his shoulder until Grandma lifted her to her feet.

"I'm afraid you'll hurt him, dear, " Grandma said when Miranda resisted.

The ambulance finally arrived. The medical technicians carefully rolled him onto a narrow metal board before lifting him onto a stretcher. Miranda followed as closely as she could as they loaded him into the ambulance. She cried when they closed the door, locking her out.

I've got to finish his work, she thought, running back to the corral. She knelt by the calf, but it was too late for it. Grandma took Miranda by the hand and led her to where Margot waited in the Subaru.

"I'll get someone to take care of the cows. We've got to see about Grandpa."

Grandma hurried to a phone as soon as they arrived at the hospital. She asked Adam to go to the dairy and finish the chores. She didn't know who else to call. Doctors and nurses were working on Grandpa and wouldn't let Miranda or Margot in to see him. Grandma asked Miranda to call her mom, Carey.

"Oh, no! What's wrong with him? How bad is he?" Mom asked, sounding terrified.

"I don't know," Miranda said and began to cry.

"I'm sorry, Miranda. I'll be right there. I'll get the next flight out, but Lorna is out of the country so I'll have to bring Kort with me."

"He just has to be okay, Mom," Miranda said as she sobbed into the phone. "I don't understand why they won't let us see him."

They had taken Grandpa to x-ray when Miranda got off the phone. She saw Elliot and Mr. Taylor walk into the emergency room.

"Elliot was going to worry himself sick so I

thought he might as well be here," Mr. Taylor told them. "Is John all right?"

"I don't know. He tries to tell me he's fine, but he's in so much pain, he looks terrible. We should know more in a few minutes," Grandma said.

Grandma's face was drawn and pale, though she tried to act brave and strong. Miranda was alarmed to see Grandma brush away tears, and even more frightened when Grandma didn't seem to notice they were running down her cheeks. Elliot sat with Margot, who was so pale that the freckles across her nose stood out like dots on white paper. Miranda sat alone on the edge of a straight chair, wishing and praying for Grandpa to be all right.

Finally, the doctor came and told them that two vertebrae in the middle of his back were shattered. One rib was broken, and the doctor said they were fortunate that it hadn't punctured a lung. When Miranda was finally allowed to see him, they had him strapped down to a strange looking bed that rotated sideways. Even his arms and legs were held down.

"Why do they have him like that?" Miranda asked in alarm. "What are they doing to him?"

"That you, Mandy? Come here. I'm okay."

"You don't look okay, Grandpa."

"They're afraid that if I move, the sharp edges and broken pieces of my bone will puncture the spinal cord. Luckily that hasn't happened. They are just making sure it doesn't by attaching me to this goofy bed. They'll do surgery tomorrow, and after that I won't have to be on this thing any more.

Mom arrived early the next day and waited with them while Grandpa was in surgery. To Miranda it seemed like forever, but she refused to go anywhere else until she saw that he was okay. Grandma offered to take her to Shady Hills, but Miranda shook her head.

As the hours dragged on, she wished that she had gone. She could have talked to Starlight. He always understood when she told him her troubles. Or at least she felt better when she thought he was listening and trying to comfort her. Instead she went into the women's rest room. It was deserted so she leaned on the long counter top and stared into the mirror.

What if Grandpa's dying? Maybe that's why it's taking so long. Maybe... but the thoughts were too sad to say out loud so she just stared at the stranger in the mirror.

It had been a long time since she had talked to the mirror child. She used to tell it all her secrets, working out her problems with the reflection that always talked back. With neither her best friend or her horse to confide in, she reverted to talking to her old friend in the mirror.

Miranda studied the ghostly white face that stared back at her. A generous sprinkling of light brown freckles peppered her fine, straight nose. Tears trickled down her cheeks and dripped off her chin.

"You're a mess," she told her reflection as she retied a pony tail in her ash blonde hair.

The girl in the mirror didn't seem to want to talk tonight, and that realization made Miranda even sadder. Was she getting too old for such imaginary games?

"I don't think I can stand it if Grandpa doesn't..." Miranda whispered leaning closer to stare into the tear-filled green eyes. They were darker to-night, almost gray. They changed colors with her moods.

"Well then, you'd better go see," the mirror child finally answered. "He's gonna be out soon."

But when Miranda saw Grandpa, his face was gray and when he tried to talk, his words trailed off into a mumble she couldn't understand.

"They had to take little slivers of bone from his leg and put them into his back bone, so that it can grow back together right," Grandma explained. "That's why it took so long for them to do the surgery. They say Grandpa will have to stay in bed for two weeks be-fore they'll let him up at all."

When he was more awake, he joked with Mom, Miranda, and Margot, telling them not to worry.

"They can't keep an old dairy farmer down. I've learned to be as ornery as my cows."

Mom said she'd stay and help out with the chores until Grandpa could come home. Adam said he'd help, too, as long as Grandpa was unable to work. As it turned out, however, Miranda did more of the work than either of them. Adam didn't know anything about milking cows, and hadn't properly cleaned and disinfected the milkers and pipelines the night of the accident. Grandma did that, with Miranda's help. When Grandma was at the hospital, where she spent most of her time, Mom left little Kort in Margot's care

in order to come help. But Margot was forgetful, and Mom ran back to check on them frequently.

"Miranda, why don't you help Margot take care of Kort for me while I help Adam," Mom said.

Miranda gladly went back to the house to play with the toddler. But soon, Mom was back to ask her a question about how things were done. They had a new milking system since Mom had grown up on the dairy. It was easier for Miranda to do it herself than to explain everything to Mom.

"You know," said Mom, when Grandma and Miranda finally came in from the barn one night, "I'm not really much help here and I need to be back in L.A. when Lorna gets back from Italy. I made a reservation to fly out at six tomorrow morning. Adam will take me. I'm going to go visit Dad tonight to tell him good-bye."

For the rest of the week, Miranda and Grandma worked together to do the main part of the chores, including the milking every morning and night. Adam fed and cleaned the barn, but he grumbled about it.

"Stupid milk cows!" Miranda heard him say. "I hope I never see another one after this ordeal is over."

Miranda checked on everything he did, sometimes finding that not all of the bucket fed calves had been fed their milk, feeder steers were not given the right feed, and the milking parlor was left far dirtier than Grandpa ever left it. She visited Grandpa every time Grandma would take her to the hospital. She brought him books and read to him, told him all about the cows, got him water and snacks, and went after nurses when he needed a pain pill.

Miranda tried to talk Grandma into letting her skip school, but there was no way. School was tiresome, in spite of Mr. Langley's interesting presentations. Miranda got up early each morning, helped with the milking, and fed the calves. She hurried home after school each day to get the cows in and help Grandma again. Margot pitched in to help feed the calves, chickens, and rabbits. On the second weekend after Grandpa's injury, they all went to Bozeman to spend the day with him.

"How's Starlight?" Grandpa asked.

"I haven't seen him all week," Miranda admitted. "I've been pretty busy, but Laurie said he's fine. She checks on him for me."

"What? Now that isn't right. I appreciate all the help you're giving your grandma, but I'm paying Adam good money to take my place while I'm laid up. You need to keep on being a kid and doing the things important to you."

"You're paying Adam?"

"Sure, he has to make a living, you know."

"I thought he was helping out just to be nice or because Mom asked him to. I should've known better," Miranda said angrily.

"Well, it shouldn't be much longer. They're going to get me up tomorrow and let me start walking up and down the halls. They have a monstrous green plastic brace for me to wear. It has a front and back and clamps around me like a turtle shell that fits too tight."

There was no school the following Monday because of a teachers' convention. Grandma drove Miranda and Margot to Shady Hills as soon as the morning chores were done. She stopped to pick up Laurie and Christopher on the way.

"Mom would have taken us, but she had to leave early this morning for a field day with the Garden Club," Laurie said.

"I didn't know your mom had joined," Miranda said. "I guess everybody changed their mind about letting her in after they found out what a good teacher your dad is."

"Well, most of them. Bill's mother quit when everyone else voted her in," Laurie said with a frown.

"Uh oh, it looks like someone's having car trouble," Grandma said, slowing the car.

"No!" Chris shouted. "There's a woman in the ditch. I think it's a wreck!"

Chapter Eleven

As soon as Grandma brought her car to a stop behind the black sedan, Miranda jumped out the door behind the driver's seat. She ran around the car in front of them. The left front fender was crumpled and the tire was off the rim. The windshield was cracked like a huge spider web. She turned as she heard Laurie's voice.

"Are you all right? Here take my jacket. You're freezing."

Laurie was putting her coat around a woman's thin shoulders.

"I'm okay. I just can't believe I had to sit here in the cold so long before anyone would stop."

"You mean people passed you by without stopping?" asked Grandma as she knelt beside the woman.

"Well, just one semi. There just wasn't any traffic. I was so scared I sat down here in the ditch and cried."

"Can you walk? We need to get you out of this wind. My car is nice and warm."

"Miranda, look at this!" Chris yelled.

Miranda continued to watch Laurie and Grandma help the woman to her feet and walk with one on each side of her to the car. Then she turned toward Chris who was staring down at a deer carcass.

"This is what she hit. Look at the size of him. Biggest buck I've seen all year."

Miranda stared at the big rack of antlers and counted the points — five on each side.

"A five point," she said. "And look how big and thick his neck is. I'm surprised a car could kill him."

"It must have hit him just right. Looks like it snapped his neck."

"Miranda! Chris! Get in the car," Grandma called. "We're taking Mrs. Meredith to the clinic."

"I'm really not hurt," the woman said. "I'm just cold and scared."

"It won't hurt to have you checked out," Grandma said. "You could be suffering hypothermia or frostbite and maybe some whiplash too. We can call your husband from there."

When they stopped in front of the clinic, Grandma told Mrs. Meredith to sit tight while she went to get a wheel chair and an attendant.

"You were such a help to me, little girl," Mrs. Meredith said as she turned around to look at Laurie. "Here's your coat. I will have to do a nice favor for you some day. Come over to my little antique shop and pick something out sometime."

"Oh, no. I don't want any pay. I just wanted to help you. Please just get well," Laurie said. "I hope you can get your car fixed."

"Don't worry about that. The insurance will take care of it. But thank you, dear. It would be nice if all children nowadays were like you."

"Do you know who that was?" Chris asked as Grandma got back in the car and pulled away from the clinic.

"I don't know, but she has the same last name as Bill," Laurie said, referring to one of their classmates. "Is she related to him?

"Yeah. That's his mother." Chris said.

Grandpa came home from the hospital on a cold windy day in mid-March. Though he couldn't be out of bed without his brace, he wouldn't stay away from the barn and feed yards. Grandma walked beside him holding on to his arm to make sure he didn't slip on the ice. At milking time, he sat on a stool in the barn and "supervised." It made the chores much more fun, for Grandpa was always cheerful, telling jokes and stories. Sometimes Miranda could talk him into singing some of his old western yodeling songs. That always made her laugh. Gradually, as he gained strength, he found chores he could do without bending his back.

"I appreciate your help more than I can tell you, Mandy," he told her, " but you must have some time with your horse every week. I'll make sure you do, I promise."

The cold weather gradually gave way to spring-like days when warm winds called chinooks or "snow eaters" blew across the land, melting the snow and coaxing green grass and early wild flowers from the thawing ground. On the Saturday following Miranda's twelfth birthday in April, Miranda, Chris, and Laurie saddled their horses, tied on their lunches and an extra coat, and headed for the river pasture. Miranda had convinced her grandparents that a day with her two best friends and their horses was the best birthday present she could have. Their parents had finally agreed to let them ride a little farther afield, as long as they were together.

"Your horse is getting awfully fat, Chris," Laurie said. "Have you been feeding her too much?"

"No," Chris said, reining Queen to a stop. "Do you think she's getting close to having her baby?"

"Oh, I forgot she was pregnant," Laurie said.

"She sure is looking like it. Funny I didn't notice it before," Miranda said. "I think you should stop riding her in the last month. Let's see, it was sometime in June when Starlight got to her. It takes eleven months for horses. I asked Grandpa. So that means she could have it some time next month."

"I think it was toward the end of June, wasn't it?" asked Chris.

"Must have been. It was after I went camping with Laurie."

"So, do you think it's okay if I keep riding her today?"

"Sure, I think so. We won't run or anything. The exercise is probably good for her," Miranda decided, proud to be consulted as if she were an expert.

Starlight pranced ahead of the other two, eager to go. Miranda sat back in the saddle, and kept tugging on the reins to keep him from running. She wished she had put a different bridle on him. She was using the bitless bridle that no one else ever seemed to use. She had always said he didn't need anything more severe, and there was no sense in hurting his mouth. Today, however, he seemed to hardly notice the pressure on his nose. He pushed his head into it, pulling the reins through her hands, giving himself more slack. Before she could take it up again, he had jumped forward into a gallop that almost unseated her. Grabbing the saddle horn, she regained her balance. When she jerked back on the reins again, he shook his head and continued to run.

"Miranda, wait!" called Laurie from behind her.

Miranda didn't try to answer. She was too busy holding on. Fighting him only made the ride rough and unpredictable. She let him have his head and concentrated on dodging tree limbs. She saw a stream ahead and braced herself for a sudden stop. But Starlight sailed over it and kept going.

"Whoa, Starlight. Easy boy. How about waiting for the others? Don't you think you're being kind of rude?" Miranda kept talking in order to quiet the horse and calm her own fears.

Then she saw the river! The warm winds had begun melting mountain snow, and the river was not only full, but swift and muddy. Chunks of ice were being tossed on the rough water along with pieces of driftwood. Starlight was heading straight for it and he wasn't slowing down.

Miranda leaned back and pulled hard on the right rein. He wasn't turning fast enough. She closed her eyes, clutched the saddle horn with all her might, and held her breath. And then Starlight put on the brakes and skidded to a stop, throwing Miranda against the saddle horn. Starlight stood calmly, as if nothing had happened, looking out over the swollen river. As Miranda got off and stood shakily beside him, he lowered his head and began cropping new sprigs of grass.

"Starlight, you scared me to death, not to mention knocking the breath out of me! Don't you ever do that again!" Miranda scolded.

He lifted his head and looked quizzically at her. Miranda laughed.

"I know what you're thinking," she said. "You look at me like I'm the crazy one. You're saying, 'What? You think I don't have sense enough to stop before diving into a cold river?' Well, you had me worried for a minute, Starlight. I thought you'd lost your mind."

"Miranda, are you all right?" called Chris and Laurie as they came trotting through the trees.

"I am now," she said. "Sorry I ran off from you. Starlight didn't give me any choice."

"Miranda I'm afraid that stallion will kill you someday. See? You can't always control him. Everyone says a stallion is not safe for kids."

"Laurie, you sound like my grandparents," Miranda said. "I'm fine. Please don't go talking about this to anyone."

"This looks like a good place to have lunch, if you two are through arguing," Chris suggested.

"We aren't arguing," Miranda and Laurie said at once. They looked at each other and laughed.

"This is a pretty spot to eat," Miranda said, "but I'm putting my coat on first. For such a sunny day, that breeze is cold."

"The ground is wet!" Laurie exclaimed as she jumped up from where she had plopped down with her lunch. "We'll have to eat standing up."

"No, let's ride back to dryer ground. I saw some rocks back a ways that we can sit on," Chris said, "and it's out of the wind."

They found the spot in a few minutes and dismounted again. They were sheltered from the wind between a steep hillside and a grove of trees. As they sat eating, Miranda looked around her.

"Hey look! See that rock formation up there? I think that's where the cave is. I bet if we followed that game trail, we could ride right up to it."

"I don't ever want to see that cave again," Chris said. "Besides, Mr. Taylor boarded up the front of it, didn't he?"

"He said he was going to. I'd like to see if he actually did or not," Miranda said. "I don't want to go down inside it, but let's ride up and see if we can still get into the big room at the opening. It could be our secret hideout."

"That hill looks pretty steep to me," Laurie said. "Are you sure the horses can make it?"

"If we zigzag back and forth like we did on our trail ride, it won't be a hard climb at all," Miranda said. "It looks easier than the other way to me. Besides, we need a secret way to get there so no one will realize we're using it for a hide out."

"What do we need a hide out for?" Chris asked.

"Oh, Chris, where's your imagination?" Miranda asked. "Just for the fun of it. We can play all kinds of games. Are you scared to ride up there?"

"No, of course not!" Chris retorted. "I just don't see the sense of it; that's all."

"What else do we have to do? It's early. We might as well be exploring," Miranda said.

"Well, I suppose. But if it gets too steep or scary, you have to promise to turn around," Laurie said.

Starlight went willingly. Miranda's only trouble was holding him back from lunging up the trail. It was easy going at first with sagebrush and a few rocks along the trail. Miranda pulled Starlight to a halt when the narrow trail disappeared under a thick juniper.

"What's the matter?" Laurie asked, stopping Lady behind Starlight.

"A tree in the way," Miranda said. "I think we can get past it by going up the bank a little ways."

She reined Starlight to the left, uphill. He scrambled over the loose dirt and rocks, but there was no level place to stop. She turned him to the right again to drop back into the path on the other side of the tree. A branch scraped her face, but she hardly noticed.

"Hey, I'm not doing that with Lady," Laurie shouted.

"I'm definitely not trying that on Queen," Chris echoed. "You said we'd take it easy with her today, Miranda."

Heat flooded Miranda's body. She couldn't see her friends, but she heard them loud and clear. In her excitement for a new adventure, she had forgotten about Queen's pregnancy. On top of that, she had gotten them all into a bad situation. She knew she'd made a big mistake.

"You're right," she shouted. "You'd better turn around. I'll come down another way and meet you at the bottom."

She could see an easier way down the slope in front of her.

"How am I supposed to turn around without falling off the path?" Chris yelled. "It's too steep here!"

"Miranda," Laurie said fearfully. "I don't like this!"

"Just wait where you are. I'll go down and circle back below you."

But when Miranda got back where she could see her friends, she was alarmed. The hillside dropped off steeply below the path, and she already knew what it was like above it. It was too narrow to turn a horse around without stepping off one way or the other.

"You'll have to back them down to a wider spot so they can turn around," Miranda said.

"I'm not going to try to ride down this thing backward," Laurie declared, stepping off her horse on the uphill side.

Holding on to Lady for balance, she walked to the front of her horse and slid back into the path. Chris did the same thing.

"How are they supposed to stay on the path when they can't see where they're going?" Chris asked.

"Just back her really slow, Chris. She'll feel her way," Miranda said, sounding more confident than she felt.

"Back, Queen. Easy girl," he said.

Chris tugged Queen's rein, bringing her chin toward her chest. Bobbing her head up and down, Queen let Chris know she didn't think this was a good idea. When Chris continued to urge her backward, she complied with her owner's command and began backing slowly. She continued for several steps with Chris gently prodding her.

"Just a little farther," Miranda coaxed. "I think the trail gets wide enough in just a few more feet."

But Queen stepped into a patch of snow and her foot slid out from under her down the hill. Her breath came out in a loud ummmph as she landed on her stomach. As she tried to push up with her other back foot, it slipped off the muddy path. Before Miranda could utter a sound, Queen was sliding downhill, scrambling in vain for footing. She struck a rock, rolled over, and picked up speed as she slid to the bottom. Miranda jumped off Starlight and skid-

ded down after her. Chris got to the bottom the same time she did.

"Queen, are you all right? Miranda, do something! She's hurt!" Chris shouted.

Chapter Twelve

Miranda slid under the mare's head, cradling it in her lap. Queen's eyes were half closed but the whites showed, making her look like she was dying. The mare's back rested against a small tree and her legs stuck out above her on an incline up the hill. There was no way she could stand up with her feet higher than her back, and the tree held her from moving. For a moment Miranda thought Queen had stopped breathing, but an occasional groan from the mare let her know she was still alive.

Miranda looked wildly around for help. She saw Laurie climbing up the hill above Lady, stopping to pull on the reins. Lady climbed after Laurie who scrambled back down to the path behind the mare. Lady was back in the path facing down hill.

"I'll go get help," Laurie called to Miranda and Chris, as she got back in the saddle.

"Have Adam bring the jeep. But first, call Doctor Talbot!" Miranda yelled.

"Why the jeep?" Chris asked. "We can't haul her in that."

"We've got to get that tree out of the way so she can get her feet back under her. I heard somewhere that a horse will die if it lies upside down too long. She sure is having a hard time breathing."

"Miranda, we've got to help her!" Chris yelled, frantically pulling on the sapling that kept the mare from rolling over. "Don't let her die!"

"Take my place, Chris. Hold her head up," Miranda ordered as she got up and ran to where Starlight was grazing. When she called his name, he came to meet her.

"I need your help, boy. I don't know if you can do this, but we have to try."

After leading him to where Queen lay, Miranda took the halter from the saddle where she'd tied it after lunch. She tied the end of the halter rope to the base of the tree where it was about two inches in diameter. She handed the halter to Chris.

"When I get on, hand this to me."

Chris scrambled up to do her bidding. Miranda climbed into the saddle, took the halter and hooked it over the saddle horn.

"Now, Starlight, let's see how much you can pull."

Starlight stopped, reared slightly, and stomped his feet when the rope tightened against the saddle.

"Wait. Back up boy. Chris, can you tighten my cinch? The saddle slipped a little."

Chris pulled the cinch as tight as he could.

"Try again, Starlight. Come on, you can do it."

When the rope tightened, Starlight stopped again.

"Starlight, pull!" Miranda yelled. Kicking his ribs for the first time ever.

Starlight backed up and then jumped forward. He groaned and lurched ahead as the tree came loose. He jumped again when he saw the tree fly toward him. He ran. Miranda screamed as the tree bounced wildly behind them, almost hitting them, and then jerking back. As Starlight jumped and swerved, it was all Miranda could do to stay on. When she regained her balance, she tugged at the halter rope. In a split second when a little slack came into the rope, Miranda pushed the halter off the horn. They were free of the phantom that seemed so bent on running them down. It took Miranda several seconds to get Starlight to slow down enough that she could control him at all. She circled him back to where Chris knelt beside Queen. She was still lying down, but her feet were under her.

"Miranda, it worked. She rolled over as soon as the tree came out, but she won't get up and she's groaning something awful," Chris exclaimed.

Miranda stared at the mare. She seemed to be in pain and she made no attempt to stand.

"I think she's in labor," Miranda said after watching Queen for a few moments.

"What?"

"Chris, I think she's having her baby. We may have to help her."

Miranda had watched her grandfather's dairy cows give birth more than once. She recognized the contractions as Queen strained and groaned, then relaxed for awhile before straining again.

"I'll look," Miranda said.

"Well?" Chris asked. "Is she?"

"I see something! A hoof. She's pushing again, and it's coming out."

"Let me see," Chris said as he crouched beside Miranda.

"Now she stopped pushing and it went back in. I don't think she should be having it yet. Maybe if we can calm her down, she'll quit pushing," said Miranda.

But another contraction had already begun. There was a hoof... and another one. They stared as a nose appeared, then a head and ears, and suddenly, the whole little body lay on the ground before them. Miranda took off her jacket and used it to wipe the filmy membrane from the foal's face and to rub it's dark body. There was a white mark on it's face. It was just like the star on Starlight's forehead, but with a streak of white extending downward from it, narrowing to a fine point a couple of inches below her eyes.

"It looks like a shooting star," she said as she rubbed it.

"Queen's trying to get up," Chris said, running back to his mare's head.

The mare struggled to her feet and quickly turned to lick her baby. The foal lay very still. Chris and Miranda were so busy watching the pair that they didn't hear the jeep until it pulled up beside them. Mr. Taylor was driving and Higgins was with him. Doctor Talbot's four wheel drive pickup was right behind it.

"The baby's not moving!" Chris yelled.

Doc Talbot stopped his truck beside them and jumped out. After examining the foal, he opened a door on the back of his pickup and turned some valves. Bending over the baby, he put the tip of some clear tubing into it's nose.

"What are you doing?" Chris asked in alarm as the doctor carefully fed the tubing farther into the little body.

"Is it going to be okay?" Miranda asked in alarm.

"Her heart is strong. I'm giving her oxygen to help her breathe," he explained. "Here, hold this a moment while I get something."

He came back with a small syringe and gave the foal a shot.

"What's that?"

"Surfactin. It's something the lungs naturally produce so that they can expand and fill with air when they are born. But if they come too early, it isn't there yet, or not completely. This may help. We'll know before long if she's going to respond. "

Everyone hovered over the small body as Doctor Talbot gently massaged her tiny body.

"What a pretty little girl. Takes after her mama, I guess," Higgins said, as the foal lifted her head.

"What do you mean?" Miranda asked.

"Her color. See how she shines in the sun. Going to be a dark sorrel, looks like to me."

"What kind of shenanigans have you kids been up to?" Mr. Taylor asked angrily. "Don't you know that stealing stud services is a federal offense?"

"But we didn't steal anything, Mr. Taylor," Miranda said.

"I keep both my stallions locked up in paddocks with high fences. The only way Queen could have been bred to my quarter horse stallion, is if you unfastened the gate and led her in!"

"But it wasn't him," Chris said.

"She's trying to get up!" Miranda exclaimed.

"That's a good sign, but let's not have her overdo it," Doctor Talbot said. "Higgins, would you ride with me and hold this filly. I want to keep the oxygen on her for awhile."

Queen pranced nervously as the men lifted her baby into the truck. Chris tried to calm the mare, but she tried to pull away from him as she nickered for her baby.

"Lead her along beside the truck, Chris. I'll drive slowly," the veterinarian ordered.

Leading Starlight, Miranda walked beside her friend.

"I think she'll be all right," Miranda said, as much to calm her own fears as to reassure Chris.

When the mare and foal were back in Queen's stall, Doctor Talbot removed the oxygen tube and steadied the foal on her spindly legs. The wobbly baby began poking her nose at her mother, looking for nourishment. He eased the little body down to the thick bedding of wood chips and went back to his truck. He came back with a bottle of yellowish liquid.

"Queen's milk hasn't come in yet. I'm going to leave a supplement for you to give the foal for a few days. It's a close match for the mother's colostrum. That's the first milk, full of antibodies to keep the baby from catching an infection. If she drinks this I think she'll be fine," the vet said as he placed the rubber nipple in the foal's mouth.

The baby's sucking reflex was strong and she emptied the bottle quickly.

"Keep an eye on her and give her another bottle

in about four hours. Give her a chance to try to nurse from her mother. As soon as she's getting enough from Queen, which won't be long, we can stop the supplemental feedings. Foals born prematurely are subject to infection, so let me know if you see any sign of trouble."

As he turned to go, he added. "Taylor, the nights are still pretty cold. You'd better put a heat lamp in the stall to keep her warm. I'll be back tomorrow."

After he left, Mr. Taylor turned to Miranda and her friends.

"You're lucky Doc got here to take care of her right away. More often than not, preemies don't make it. Now, I want an explanation. You say you didn't steal stud services. Do you mean you had her bred somewhere else?" Mr. Taylor asked. "If so, why? I might have given you a break on the price if you'd told me you wanted her bred."

"No. We didn't plan it. It was an accident. Queen got away from us one day," Miranda said.

"Got away where? There are no other stallions anywhere near here," Mr. Taylor said. "Dot's Dash, my quarter horse, is the only sorrel stud for miles around, and I know he couldn't have gotten to her unless someone purposely opened the gate and put her in with him."

"It was Starlight."

"That's impossible!" Mr. Taylor shouted. "Don't lie to me. I'm not stupid. Some things are scientifically impossible, and this is one of them."

"She wasn't with any horse but Starlight!"

Miranda said, angry at being called a liar. "If she was, we would say so. We're not stupid either."

"Starlight can't be the father! Black is a dominant color. Starlight is homozygous for black."

"I don't know what that word means, but I know what I saw. Chris and I watched it happen. We were both riding Queen, and Starlight started chasing her so we jumped off. They went up on the hill and...did it," Miranda said defensively.

"Well, there must have been another time. Starlight can't produce sorrel foals. That's why I'm using him to replace Knight as my Thoroughbred stallion."

"Maybe you should get Talbot to take some blood samples, Cash," Higgins said. "A DNA test can settle this argument easily enough."

"I will not!" Taylor said. "I know genetic facts."

"Let's name her Shooting Star," Chris said after Mr. Taylor stormed away.

"You two sound like you're naming your baby," Laurie said laughing. "You make a sweet mommy and daddy."

"That's not funny!" Chris said.

"In a way, we are her parents," Miranda said. "Chris's mare is the mother, and my stallion is the dad. That makes her belong to both of us, doesn't it?"

"I guess so," Chris admitted. "I just hope my dad doesn't make me sell her. I don't think he'll be too happy about her having a baby."

"If he does, I'll talk my grandpa into helping me buy your share. You can still help take care of her."

"All right, mama and papa," Laurie said, laughing again, "what's her name going to be?"

"Shooting Star," Chris and Miranda said together.

Being born early, Shooting Star was thin and delicate. Doctor Talbot stopped by each morning for the first week to check on her. Within two days, Queen had plenty of milk, and Shooting Star nursed eagerly between naps. Between Chris, Miranda, and Laurie, she never lacked attention.

Miranda wasn't allowed to ride Starlight because Mr. Taylor had moved him to Knight's old paddock, and turned the old stallion out in the grassy hill pasture. Starlight now had a harem of mares and fillies. Sometimes when she went to visit him, he didn't seem to have time for her. At other times he nuzzled her pockets, looking for treats. She fed him and brushed him, and took him out for a half hour each day to exercise him.

She hated not being able to ride him in the pasture or race him on the track, but it gave her a chance to play with Shooting Star. She was beautiful, with a white stocking on her back right leg, and a shorter white sock on the left front. Her forehead seemed too big, but Doctor Talbot told her it was from being premature and that she would gradually lose the unnatural bulge. Her spindly legs looked like stilts and she sometimes tripped over them. She quickly became a pet, running and jumping as best she could toward the kids whenever they entered the paddock. Queen got lots of treats and loving care too.

When Shooting Star was three weeks old, Mr. Taylor was waiting for Miranda when she arrived at Shady Hills after school. When she stepped out of the Bergman's station wagon, her stomach did a flip-flop, as she met the old man's stormy face.

"Miranda, come to the house. I need to talk to you," he said in a cold, harsh voice.

Chris and Laurie looked at her questioningly.

"What did you do?" Chris asked as Mr. Taylor turned and strode toward his house.

"Want us to come with you?" offered Laurie.

"I don't know what I did, but I'd better go alone, or he'll have something else to be mad about."

Chapter Thirteen

Mr. Taylor was waiting at the kitchen door and ushered her inside.

"Sit down," he said, pointing to a chair at the kitchen table. He sat down across from her.

"I brought the fillies in from the hill pasture a couple of weeks ago. I separated the quarter horses from the thoroughbreds and then put them in with the studs; the quarter horses with Dot's Dash and the Thoroughbred fillies with Starlight."

"I know," Miranda said.

"Well, this morning one of the quarter horse fillies had a foal by her side." Mr. Taylor paused and glared at Miranda.

Miranda stared back, confused, but beginning to see where this was going.

"Can you guess what color it was?"

Miranda shrugged. "Black?"

"I thought so at first, but looking more closely,

I see a lot of bay hair on his legs, face, and belly. It's going to be bay. Now my stallions are known for breeding true. It's what gives this ranch it's value. When a man brings his mare to have her bred to Cadillac's Last Knight, he knows he is going to get a pure black foal. Sorrel isn't dominant, so Dot's Dash can't always throw a sorrel foal. But I don't believe Dash is the sire. He hasn't been out of his paddock in years. Do you understand what I'm saying?"

"Not really. We just started studying genetics in school, but I haven't learned those words yet."

"Well, it boils down to this: I think you might know something about who sired the bay colt out there. And there's another filly that looks like she could drop a foal any day. I don't breed my fillies until they are three, and then only certain ones. How did these two get pregnant a year too soon?"

Miranda lowered her head and swallowed hard. This would have been easier if she'd told Mr. Taylor right away when it happened last year. She could see that now.

"Chris and I decided to take our lunch up on the hill pasture to eat. I took Starlight along to get him used to the saddle, but I rode behind Chris on Queen. Starlight started chasing Queen, so we got off as soon as we could. That's when she got bred. Later that day, Starlight got away from me again and ran back into the hill pasture. He found the fillies before I could catch him."

"That's the same story Higgins told me. It just doesn't make sense," Mr. Taylor said as he rubbed his jaw. "I guess I'll have to order that DNA test after all. Cadillac's Last Knight is Starlight's sire. His mother was Black Jetta, who got her name from her color. I didn't own her, but I bought her foal. She was one of the fastest race horses at that time. I saw her papers and both her parents were black, but there must have been one recessive gene that carried all the way down to Starlight."

Miranda stared at Mr. Taylor who looked like he had just lost his best friend.

"Well, let's go get him and put him back in his own paddock. It's too bad I didn't find this out before I put the fillies in with him," Mr. Taylor grumbled.

Miranda rolled her eyes, but made no comment.

As they walked out the door, a very fancy horse van pulled by a matching pickup with California license plates, crossed the cattle guard. The driver stopped in front of Mr. Taylor.

"I've got Ebon's Dark Shadow here. Where do you want her?"

Miranda recognized the name from the race in California. This was the black mare that beat Fancy by a length. Miranda had tried to persuade Mr. Taylor to buy her.

"Uh, there's a bit of a misunderstanding I'll have to work out with the owner before I put her with the stud," Mr. Taylor said.

"Look, I can't wait. She's close to the end of her cycle by now. If she isn't bred soon, it will be too late. I'm supposed to wait while she's bred and then start back with her."

"I'll go call the owners while you unload her. I'll be right back."

Miranda watched as the sleek, high strung mare was led from the trailer. She wore a blanket and a matching hood of some kind on her face. It had holes for her eyes but they had blinders to keep her from seeing sideways. The driver was getting very impatient as he stood holding her.

"May I walk her for you?" Miranda asked.

"Maybe you could take me to Sir Jet or Starlight or whatever his name is. I want to get this over with and get back to civilization."

"I think we'd better wait for Mr. Taylor," Miranda said.

Soon he emerged from the house, striding quickly toward the waiting driver.

"Well, I've made a deal with the owners. We'll breed her to Cadillac's Last Knight. In the meantime, I'll have my vet run a DNA test on her. If she tests homozygous for black, I'm buying her. If not, you can take her back with you."

"But how long will that take? I can't wait around here overnight!" the driver protested.

"It'll take a few days to get the results back from the lab. We'll leave her with Knight in the meantime. Miranda, see if you can get Starlight out of Knight's paddock while I go get Knight from the pasture."

"Hey, wait a minute!" shouted the driver, but Miranda was already running toward Starlight.

Blood tests proved that Starlight was indeed the sire to three foals that spring: Shooting Star, the bay colt and a black filly. His DNA had one gene for the color black and one for sorrel. This made him worthless as a stud in Mr. Taylor's eyes. The reputation for this ranch was built on the ability to produce black foals. The DNA test from Ebon's Dark Shadow gave the result Mr. Taylor was hoping for. Any offspring of her's and Knights would be homozygous for black. Mr. Taylor hoped she'd have a colt who would be a winner on the race track. Even so, he'd have to wait a couple more years to retire Last Knight and let him have a well earned rest in green pastures.

Miranda thought Mr. Taylor was putting far too much importance on the color of his horses, even though she loved black. She thought that Starlight was the most beautiful horse in the world. Shadow, the new mare, was striking in her sleek, shiny black coat. But all the other horses on the ranch were pretty too, especially Queen, Sunny, Fancy and most of all, Shooting Star. She was just glad that Starlight was no longer the focus of Mr. Taylor's racing and breeding program. It allowed her more time with him. She was in his stall, brushing his already shining coat when she overheard Mr. Taylor talking to Higgins.

"I think we ought to get Talbot to cut Starlight," Miranda heard Mr. Taylor say. "He's no longer needed for breeding, and it will make him a safer horse for Miranda to ride."

Miranda burst out of Starlight's stable and strode toward Mr. Taylor and Higgins.

"What are you talking about? You're planning something against Starlight, aren't you? He's half mine, remember? You can't do anything unless I agree too!" she exclaimed.

"Hold on, there. We aren't going to hurt him. I was just saying, I think it would be a good idea to have him gelded so that he'll be a better horse for you," Mr. Taylor said.

"A better horse? He's already the best horse in the world. Do you think you can make him better by taking away part of him? I won't let you hurt him!"

"Miranda, be reasonable. Most of the male horses on this place are gelded. It isn't practical to keep a horse a stallion except for breeding purposes," Mr. Taylor argued.

Growing up on a dairy farm, Miranda was well aware of the practice of castrating baby bulls to make them more docile, easier to fatten, and unable to reproduce. She hated it and secretly cried when she heard them bellow in pain at the quick operation.

"You can't do it if I say you can't. He's half mine!" Miranda said stubbornly.

"You are a minor. The decision will be mine and your guardians', whether you like it or not. I'm sure they'll be happy to have it done for your safety. It's a miracle you haven't been hurt before. I'm not sure your family wouldn't sue me, if something did happen to you on that horse!"

"My family isn't like that!" Miranda shouted, her anger overcoming all caution. "That's all you ever care about, isn't it? I should have known this was about money. Well, my grandparents won't let you do this. If you're afraid they'll sue you, sell me your half. I'll even take him off your ranch."

"Maybe you don't know what your parents want. Adam says your mother would have a fit if she knew you were riding that horse. But, it's not about the money," Mr. Taylor hastened to add. "I don't want you to get hurt or worse killed. I'd be..."

"Adam?" Miranda interrupted when she found her voice. "What does he have to do with this? I should have known he would think of another way to ruin my life!"

She felt tears filling her eyes and her chest hurt. Unwilling to let the men see her cry, she turned and fled to the hayloft of the old barn. She plopped down in a pile of hay and cried until there were no tears left. When Adam came back to Shady Hills, Miranda hoped it meant an end to her Mom's engagement. But it wasn't. The wedding was still on. According to Mom, she and Adam had decided it would be better for Adam to be near the girls to "form a bond." Mom wanted them to all live together after the wedding. Thinking of this brought a fresh wave of tears. When she finally quit sobbing, she heard voices.

"What are you doing up here?" Miranda demanded, sitting up.

"We were here when you came up the ladder," Margot replied. "What were you crying about?"

"We didn't mean to spy on you," Elliot said. "We were swinging on the rope and jumping into that hay pile. We quit so we wouldn't land on you."

"I hear a car honking," Margot said. "I think Grandma's here to take us home."

There was a message for Miranda to call Mom as soon as she got home.

"I've decided to have my wedding in Montana on the front lawn of Grandma's house. It's less than a month away. I have the dresses made for you and Margot, but I need to make sure they fit. You will be my attendants," Mom said, excitedly. "There are so many arrangements that I can't make from here. I have permission to bring Kort with me, so I can stay there until the wedding. We'll be flying in next week!"

Miranda was stunned. It made the wedding seem so soon.

"You're still planning on getting married in June?" she managed to ask.

"Of course! Were you expecting me to change my mind?"

"I can hope, can't I?" Miranda muttered.

"Did you say what I think you said?" Mom asked. "Look, Miranda. I know you don't like everything about Adam. But I have to think of my own life. I'm tired of being single. Doesn't that matter to you?"

"Sorry, Mom," Miranda said. "I'll see ya next week."

"I can hardly wait. I miss you," Mom said. "I'm sure you'll come to love Adam once you really know him. You'll see."

Miranda knew better. The more she was around Adam Barber, the more she disliked him. Even his own daughter didn't seem to like him. Why couldn't Mom see him the way they did before it was too late?

"Grandpa, could we keep Starlight here?" Miranda asked at the supper table that evening. "He's half mine, and I think Mr. Taylor might let me buy his half."

"I'm afraid you can't afford to buy his half, and neither can I," Grandpa answered. "But why would you want him here? You see him almost every day as it is. Your friends' horses are there. You wouldn't be able to ride with them if he was here."

"I want him where I can watch over him. I don't think he's safe."

"Not safe? Why?"

"Mr. Taylor is talking about having Dr. Talbot geld him. He said he can do it without my permission," Miranda said. "You wouldn't let him do that, would you Grandpa? If he asks you, please say, no."

"Grandma and I have wished he was gelded ever since we found out you were riding him," Grandpa said. "We knew he was valuable to Mr. Taylor as a stud, so we never suggested it. If Mr. Taylor has changed his mind, it might be a good idea."

Miranda stared at her grandpa in disbelief. How could he turn on her like this? She blinked back tears, trying to speak without crying.

"Don't get any ideas about trying to steal him away in the night and hide him again," Grandma said, lifting Miranda's chin and looking her in the eye. "Promise me!"

"It's not fair! How can everyone be against me and Starlight? And now you're making me promise not to try to protect my own horse!"

"Mandy, calm down," Grandpa said, gently, using the nickname that usually softened her anger. "It's a simple operation. Dr. Talbot has done thousands of them. Starlight will be sore for a couple of days, and then he'll be just fine again."

"Please, Grandpa! Please promise you won't let them do it. I like Starlight the way he is. It will change him. He's still valuable for breeding, no matter what Mr. Taylor thinks. We could start our own horse ranch right here."

"I think I'll stick to cows," Grandpa said with a chuckle. "We'll talk about this some more before I make any decision. I'm sure you'll come to realize that it will be better for you if we have it done."

Chapter Fourteen

Miranda hurried to Starlight's stall every day she could get to Shady Hills. When she couldn't, she asked her friends or Margot to make sure he had not been hurt while she was away. She could hardly wait for the last day of school, so she could spend every single day with him. But Mom arrived a week before the end of school and demanded that Miranda hurry home to have alterations done to her dress.

Miranda thought the peach colored chiffon with the fuzzy white flowers all over it was hideous. She tried to talk her mother into finding something else, but it matched Margot's, and Mom liked it. It was too wide across the shoulders, chest, around the waist, and about two inches too short. Margot's fit perfectly, so she was allowed to ride Elliot's bus to his house after school so she could play with him.

"Please, check on Starlight for me?" Miranda begged as Margot got on the bus. "Here, take this apple and cut it up for him. Elliot will let you use his knife."

"Okay," Margot said. "I'm sorry you can't go."

"I don't know what to do about the length, do you?" Mom asked Grandma as Miranda stood on a stool in the middle of the kitchen floor.

"We could get some wide white lace that would match the flocking on the dress and add a ruffle," Grandma said.

"That would be pretty." Mom agreed. "We could use matching lace to fill in the neck line where it's too low."

"It's frilly enough," Miranda objected. "Why can't I wear black jeans and a silk shirt. Then I'd match the guys and it wouldn't matter."

"Don't be silly, Miranda," Mom said sternly. "This is my wedding, and I won't have you looking like a boy, no matter how much you hate dresses. It won't hurt you to dress up one day for me."

Tears sprung to Miranda's eyes and she clamped her jaws shut tightly to keep from saying things that would only make her mother more angry.

By the time Mom and Grandma finished tucking and pinning, it was chore time. Miranda was glad to put her jeans back on and get out of the house. She called Little Brother and headed for the pasture to bring the cows in. When she got back to the barn, she stayed close to her grandfather. He was doing more work every day as he got stronger and learned to maneuver in spite of the tight back brace. Miranda helped him in every way she could. Finally, the first six cows were in the barn, and Grandpa had the milkers on all of them.

"Grandpa," Miranda said, as Grandpa relaxed for a moment, "I've been thinking."

"Yes?"

"If we had Starlight here, I could use him for getting the cows in every night, and whenever you needed to sort some out, or wean some calves, we'd have a horse to use."

"We've been getting along pretty well on foot, it seems to me," Grandpa answered.

"I know, but sometimes it would be easier if we had a horse. Besides, you wouldn't have to take me to Shady Hills all the time. I think Mr. Taylor would let us bring him here if you asked him."

"You're worried that Mr. Taylor is going to have him gelded when you aren't there," Grandpa said. "Is that it?"

"Yes," Miranda admitted as Grandpa went to take off another milker.

Miranda hurried to open the stanchions of the cows that were done and pour grain for the next group. When the barn was emptied, she opened the door and let the next six cows come in. She washed their udders with a disinfectant solution, and Grandpa put the milkers on.

"Mandy," Grandpa said gently, "I gave you my word that I would tell Mr. Taylor not to do that yet. I've always been worried about you getting hurt, but you've been faithful about wearing your helmet and obeying the rules, so I let you take the chance. I'd feel better if he were a gentle gelding rather than a spirited stallion, but I don't know if gelding him now would make that much difference."

Miranda held her breath as she listened, her whole body tense.

"The point is," Grandpa went on, "I gave you my word. Mr. Taylor won't do anything without my consent, and I hope you know I would never go behind your back. Months ago, I signed a waiver, releasing Taylor of all responsibility in case of an accident. He has everyone who boards or rides horses there sign one. So, maybe he isn't worried about being sued. Maybe he's concerned about you."

Miranda was overcome with emotion and tried to hug her grandfather in the bulky plastic brace.

"Thank you," she whispered.

Grandma drove Miranda and Margot to Shady Hills as soon as the chores were done the next morning. Miranda rushed to Starlight's stall. He seemed as happy to see her as she was him. She put his halter on him and led him over to Queen's paddock.

"Come see your baby, Starlight. Isn't she the prettiest little thing you ever saw?"

Starlight sniffed the little filly who came wobbling toward Miranda as soon as they came through the gate. They touched noses and Shooting Star nibbled Starlight's lip. He snorted and she squealed, turned and bucked, and then came back for more. Miranda laughed at them. Queen trotted up to make sure her baby was not being mistreated. Starlight immediately lost interest in the foal, arched his neck and nipped at Queen.

"Oh, no. This was not a good idea, was it," Miranda said, tugging on Starlight's rope and pulling him toward the gate.

With a quick toss of his head, he jerked the rope from Miranda's hand, leaving it stinging.

"Oh, well, little Star," Miranda said, nudging the foal into the stable. "We'll just stay out of the way and let nature take it's course."

She closed the lower door so that Shooting Star couldn't get out. Miranda was afraid Starlight might step on the tiny foal while he chased Queen, who was obviously in heat. Miranda heard a car pull up in front of the stable. She looked out to see Chris and Laurie get out of Langley's car.

"Chris, I hope you want another foal, because if you don't, it's probably too late now!" she exclaimed when her friends entered Queen's stall.

"What are you talking about?" he asked.

"I should have known better," Miranda said. "I took Starlight to see his baby, and, well, he was more interested in Queen. He got away from me again."

"It's okay," Chris said, laughing. "I don't think Dad will mind. Mom thinks Shooting Star is cute, and Dad thinks she may be worth a lot of money, so neither one of them seems to mind."

"We can't sell her, ever!" Miranda exclaimed. "If you want to sell your share, I'll buy it. And then there's Mr. Taylor. We owe him half the stud fee."

"Yeah, and I suppose he'll say the same thing if Queen has another one. The trouble is, neither you or

I have the money. I don't want to sell Shooting Star either, but we'll have to wait and see."

"You two are so lucky," Laurie said. "I sure wish Lady would have a foal."

"Yeah, I guess she's just too old," Miranda said. "I'm sorry, I wish she would."

"I think you can get your horse, now, Miranda," Chris said as he looked out into the paddock. "It looks like he's lost interest, at least for the moment."

Miranda hurried out to get him while Chris and Laurie walked Shooting Star back to her mother.

"Let's go for a ride," Miranda suggested. "It's a beautiful day. We haven't ridden in the river pasture since Shooting Star was born."

"Miranda, I can't ride Queen around Starlight. We already know what happens when she's in heat! Besides, I think Shooting Star is too little to go very far."

"Maybe Mr. Taylor would let you ride one of his horses. And maybe Elliot and Margot would like to go."

But Margot didn't want to ride. She and Elliot were building a fort out of hay bales in the old barn.

"Come play with us. It's lots of fun," Margot said, and Elliot seconded the invitation.

"Thanks, but I want to ride," Miranda said.

"You and Laurie go. This looks like fun. I'll stay with the kids," Chris said, as if he were a grownup.

Laurie had Lady saddled and ready to go first, because Miranda wanted to longe Starlight. He was full of energy, and it was hard to get him to settle down and obey voice commands. Finally she decided he was ready.

"What's the matter with Lady," Laurie asked as they headed down the lane toward the river pasture.. "I think Starlight's energy is contagious."

"Laurie, stop and get off!" Miranda shouted. "I can't control him. He wants to come after her. "

Miranda swung out of the saddle and dropped to the ground. Holding Starlight's reins firmly, she pulled him around so his back was to Lady and wrapped the reins around a tree. He jerked back, snapping the reins. Wheeling, he lowered his head and nipped at Lady's heels. Laurie jumped out of the way and the horses disappeared into the trees.

"Miranda, I told you he was too wild!" Laurie said, as tears welled into her eyes. "We could have been killed."

"He only gets this way when he's around a mare in heat. Maybe Lady will have a baby after all."

Laurie gradually calmed down as they trudged through the pasture looking for their horses.

"Remember how we used to put Lady in the round pen and then bring Starlight over to make sure he wasn't interested," Miranda asked Laurie.

"Yeah. We quit doing that a long time ago because she never came into season and we didn't think she could."

"I bet we never make that mistake again," Miranda said, laughing.

"It's not funny!" Laurie exclaimed. "I was so scared, I thought I'd die. But if she gets pregnant, it'll be worth it."

They finally caught up with the horses, who were now standing peacefully together, nibbling grass. Miranda took the halter she had tied to Starlight's saddle and put it on him. She tied him to a tree while Laurie mounted Lady and started back toward the

stables. They weren't taking any more chances.

After supper, Mom insisted that Miranda try on her dress for the wedding. Miranda groaned, but did as she was told.

"Turn," Mom commanded.

Miranda slowly pivoted as both Mom and Grandma beamed at her.

"You look like an angel! It's beautiful, Miranda, honest," Mom said proudly.

Miranda felt foolish as she looked down at the white lacy ruffles across her chest, and at the bottom of the full skirt that now touched the floor.

"May I please take it...," she began.

But a loud knock on the door interrupted her.

"Who would be coming at this hour," Mom asked. "Maybe it's Adam, though he doesn't usually knock."

She opened the door to a tall, thin man. It wasn't Adam.

Chapter Fifteen

Mom stepped back, hand on her chest, and sat down on the nearest chair. Her face was so pale that Miranda thought she was going to faint.

"Do you mind if I come in?" the stranger asked as he took one step into the living room.

Now Miranda could see his narrow, suntanned face under wavy light brown hair. He twisted a ball cap in his hands. Then his soft green eyes met hers. Her heart thudded in her chest. She couldn't move.

"Barry?" Grandma asked.

He nodded and a half smile turned up the corner of his mouth.

"My good heavens! Come in and sit down. We all thought you were dead!"

"Is this my daughter?" he asked hesitantly as he continued to stare at Miranda.

Miranda looked down at her frilly dress and her face turned red. Turning away from the stranger's gaze, she ran from the room.

Tears streamed down her face as she struggled out of the dress and put her jeans and T-shirt back on. Margot stood in the doorway watching her.

"What's the matter, Miranda? Who is that man out there?"

"I think it's my father."

"Is that bad? Why are you crying?"

"I don't know. I always dreamed of him coming back. I just never really believed...," she hesitated, tossing the dress on the bed. "I sure didn't want him to see me in this!"

As she crept back into the living room, Barry was sitting on the edge of Grandpa's recliner. Mom was on the floor in front of him, tears in her eyes.

"I'm sorry, Carey. It was wrong for me to show up this way. I should have called or written. I guess I was afraid you'd tell me not to come. I had to see you again, and meet my child. But I think I frightened her."

"I'm Miranda Stevens," Miranda said, crossing the room quickly to stand in front of him. "Are you really my dad?"

"Yes, I am. I was a fool to leave, and I hope you'll forgive me. I started to write you a letter once. Things happened, but I came back as soon as I could."

Miranda held out a folded piece of paper. "This is the letter you started. Adam gave it to me last year. I keep it under my pillow all the time. When I can't sleep, I take it out and read it."

"So Barber did find you! I didn't even know if he was alive or not. I haven't been able to find out much of anything," Barry said, reverently touching the letter. "I'm glad to know this reached you, and that it means so much. I haven't been a decent father. But I've had a lot of years to think about the kind I want to be. I hope I'll have the chance."

He looked at Mom and she looked at the floor.

"Please excuse me," Mom said, getting up and hurrying from the room.

"Maybe I'm too late," Barry said sadly, to no one in particular. "That was a very fancy dress you had on when I came in."

"I hate the ugly thing!" Miranda exclaimed. "I'm supposed to wear it in Mom's wedding."

"Your mother's getting married?"

"To Adam; in two weeks," Miranda said.

"Oh," Barry said, as if he'd been hit in the stomach. "Well, I knew I couldn't expect her to wait all these years. I thought she might already be married. Maybe she has been. Is this your sister and brother?" he asked, looking toward the hallway where Margot stood holding Kort, who had just awakened.

"No, Margot is Adam's daughter. So she'll be my sister after Mom and Adam get married. That's the only thing good about it. Kort is a boy Mom takes care of for a fashion model in California."

Barry nodded at them, but Margot didn't venture any farther into the room. After an awkward silence Barry stood up.

"I guess I'd better go, then," he said slowly. Turning to Grandma, he asked, "I guess legally, Carey and I aren't married anymore?"

"Well, we thought you were dead. No action was ever taken, so I don't know. We'll have to look into it."

"May I come back?" Barry asked as he opened the door.

"Yes!" Miranda shouted, running to him and wrapping her arms around his waist. "Please don't leave again. I want my daddy back!"

He picked her up and held her tightly as she pressed her face into his neck, wetting it with her tears.

"Please come for supper tomorrow, Barry. Johnny will want to see you," Grandma said, referring to Grandpa. "He went to bed early tonight, but I know he — all of us — want to hear what happened and where you've been all these years."

Mom was in the "spare room," a remodeled back porch that had once been Corey's. Miranda knocked on the door and waited. There was no answer for a minute, but finally Mom opened it a crack, then wider to let Miranda in. Mom's red eyes and blotched mascara showed that she had been crying.

Miranda had planned a speech about how Mom owed her the chance to get to know her father; that she should forget about Adam until she got to know Barry again. But she couldn't say anything in the face of her mother's tears. Instead, Miranda put her arms around her mom and let her own tears fall again. They held each other for a long time before Miranda pulled back and looked into her Mom's eyes.

"What now, Mom?"

"I don't know, baby. I'm so confused," Mom

said. "You have no idea how it felt to see Barry again. So many mixed up emotions that I don't know what I'm feeling."

"I like how my daddy looks, Mom. He seems like the kind of dad I always wanted."

"You know all that from seeing him for ten minutes?" Mom asked with a forced little laugh. "Well, I like the way he looks too, but it's too soon to tell what kind of father he might turn out to be. He has a lot of explaining to do."

"I know. Grandma asked him to come for supper tomorrow, so he can tell us what happened."

"Oh great!" Mom exclaimed sarcastically. "Adam will be here too. That should be interesting."

Grandpa was up early, and so was Miranda. She couldn't wait to tell him about Barry Stevens' miraculous return, but he'd already heard about it from Grandma.

"I hope he'll stay around close," she told Grandpa. "Maybe you could hire him to help on the dairy. Adam doesn't like doing it."

"Oh, he doesn't, eh?" Grandpa asked with a laugh. "Don't you think we'd better find out what your father has in mind before we start twisting his arm to work for us?"

"Well, sure, I just mean, you know, in case he wants to."

"It's amazing. A hero back from the dead, and not one of you thought to ask him how that happened," Grandpa said with a grin. "I'm looking forward to some very fascinating stories tonight."

"Your grandpa always had a soft spot for Barry. I think he was almost as devastated as I was when he left," Mom told Miranda as they prepared supper together. Miranda looked at her sharply and saw that she was fighting back tears.

When supper was ready and the table set with the "good" dishes, Grandpa, Grandma, and Adam came in from finishing the milking and feeding. As Adam washed up at the kitchen sink, and Grandma went to the bathroom to freshen up, Miranda ran to tell Margot they were ready to eat as soon as their guest arrived. Margot wasn't in their room, so Miranda looked in the spare room, where Kort was taking a late nap. She wasn't there either.

"Has anyone seen Margot," she asked. "I can't find her."

"She was outside with that big black dog before I started feeding," Adam said. "I haven't seen her since."

Miranda went outside and called Little Brother. He didn't come bounding to her call as he usually did. A car turned into the driveway and stopped. That usually brought Little Brother to the scene, barking fiercely as he wagged his tail. This time, he didn't come.

Miranda ran to the car as her father stepped out and stood before her. He squatted down to her level and smiled. Opening his arms to her, he said, "Just as I thought, my daughter is beautiful. Prettier even than I could imagine. I can hardly wait to get to know you, Miranda."

"Me too," she said, leaning into his welcoming arms. "I missed you."

"Me too," he whispered.

"Oh, everyone is waiting to eat," Miranda said, remembering. "Except Margot. I was looking for her."

"May I help you?" he asked.

"Barry, is that you?" Grandma called from the front door. "Come on in. Johnny wants to see you."

"Go ahead," Miranda said. "I'll find Margot so we can eat."

Miranda went to all the places where she and Margot liked to play or explore, but found nothing. Finally, far behind the barn and corrals in the hay barn, a muffled bark answered Miranda's call.

"Margot, are you in there?" Miranda asked, climbing hay bales like stairs.

"I don't want any supper," Margot said from somewhere in the shadows.

"Why not? Are you afraid of my dad?"

"No."

"What then?" Miranda asked as she sat down beside Margot on the top tier of hay under the rafters.

Margot shrugged.

"Come on! We said we'd tell each other things, remember?"

"Well," Margot began reluctantly. "Now that your dad is here, your mom won't marry my dad, and I don't know what will happen to me."

"Why, I suppose you'll just go on staying here with us," Miranda said.

"What if your mom and dad get back together

and you all go off somewhere else to live? What if my dad takes me far away where I don't know anyone?"

"I, I don't know. I hadn't thought about any of us leaving here. I know I don't want to, but like Grandpa says, we don't know what my father's plans are," Miranda admitted, suddenly worried. "I know what let's do! Hold my hands and let's go where we can see the sky."

"Why?"

"Well, it's almost dark enough to see the first star. I think if you wish on it, dreams will come true."

"Shooting stars work too," Margot said as they surveyed the sky which was still devoid of stars of any kind.

"That's right! All we have to do is close our eyes and think of Shooting Star and make our wish."

"The baby horse, Shooting Star?"

"Yes, can you picture her?"

"Sure, let's do it."

When everyone finally sat down to eat, Mom complained that supper was ruined because everything had gotten cold and had to be reheated. Miranda had never seen her so uptight. She looked from one man to the other and tried to force a casual conversation between them.

When the meal was finally over, the table cleared, and the kitchen cleaned up, they all moved to the living room gathering around Grandpa's recliner.

"Well, Barry, we know you were in the navy with Adam. He told us the story of how fire broke out on the aircraft carrier in the middle of the Atlantic. You tried to save a man who was burning and both you and the victim were washed overboard, never to be seen again," Grandpa said, summarizing. "But here you are, after we all thought you'd been dead for years. How did you survive, and where have you been?"

Chapter Sixteen

Barry cleared his throat and began, "The storm was fierce, and we both went under for a long time. At first A.J. panicked and kept pushing me down to try to get out. I punched him and held him at arm's length. When we surfaced he kept struggling until I said, 'A.J. if you don't quit that, I'm going to have to hit you, and leave you here alone.' That brought him to his senses. We kept treading water looking for something to hold onto. We were both good swimmers, but we held on to each other so we wouldn't get separated. The waves were like mountains. If one of those came up between us, we'd never see each other again. We glimpsed the lights on the ship once in awhile, but then they'd disappear behind a wall of water again. I guess the guys on board were throwing life savers out into the dark, because one of them hit us and we grabbed on. We thought we'd get pulled back on board, but the line snapped and after that we never saw the ship again."

The room was completely silent when Barry paused to take a breath. When no one said anything, he continued.

"It took all our strength to hang on to that one little buoy, but we never let go. Daylight finally came, but the wind and rain kept on, so that you could hardly tell. I don't know how long it was before it died down and the waters became calmer. I know we were both blue and shaking all over by the time the sun came out. Then we took turns sleeping, so one of us could stay awake to make sure the other one wouldn't lose his grip and go under. I did that once, but woke up and grabbed on again. Once we relaxed from fighting the waves, the chills weren't quite as bad and we could sleep a little."

"A.J.," Adam said when Barry paused again. "Aaron Jenkins. I'd forgotten the guy's name. Is he still alive?"

"Alive and well! Married and living on a cattle ranch in Australia," Barry said.

"Australia? How did he get there?" Adam asked.

"After three days, a small freighter came by and spotted us. They took us aboard and gave us food, water, and dry clothes. We thought we were in heaven for awhile, after thinking we were going to die out there in the middle of the ocean. But it was a filthy little vessel, and their supplies were limited. We worked along with the rest of the crew to keep the thing running. The engine was old and worn out, and they didn't have any mechanics on board. Without us, they wouldn't have made it as far as they did. We came within sight of a harbor. I still don't know which one. They lowered anchor, but the captain wouldn't let us go ashore with them. He said he needed us to get the rest of the way to Australia, where they were delivering cargo."

"How could they keep you on board, if you wanted off?" Miranda asked again.

"They had guns and didn't look like they would mind using them. Four men were left to guard us, while the captain and some others took a list of parts we needed for the engine repair and went to get supplies. We both sent letters we'd written home and asked them to mail them for us. Of course we didn't think they would.

"It took us a month to get the thing up and running again. I kept thinking I'd find a chance to get to shore, but they were very vigilant. They didn't trust us, that's for sure. It took another six or seven months to get to Australia. The thing was slow and kept breaking down. When we pulled into Sydney, they finally let us go ashore, but watched us like a hawk. They wanted to keep us for the trip back.

"Before that could happen, the captain and all the crew was arrested for smuggling illegal drugs into the country. A.J. and I tried to tell them that we were not part of the crew and had nothing to do with it, but it was our word against theirs, so we were thrown in the slammer for four years."

"Couldn't you prove you were in the navy or

get the U. S. government to vouch for you?" asked Grandpa.

"We tried telling them, but our captors had disposed of the uniforms we were wearing along with our dog tags and everything we had in our pockets. We had no way of identifying ourselves. After we'd served our time, we went to the U.S. embassy and gave them our names and serial numbers. They looked it up and told us we were dead.

"'Obviously we're not,' I said and I asked them to clear it up, report to our families that we were alive and help us get back to the states. Well, once the government goes to all the paper work to declare somebody dead, they aren't in any hurry to go through all the red tape it would take to bring them back to life."

"Why didn't the navy ever notify us that you were dead?" Mom asked. "For more than ten long years I believed you were alive, and away from Miranda and me because you didn't want us. At least the news Adam brought that you'd died finally brought some closure."

"That was my fault," Barry said, hanging his head. "I never told the navy I was married, so I didn't give them your name. The only address they had for me was my old one back east. And none of my aunts or uncles there knew that I was married."

"You sure weren't very proud of us, were you?" Mom asked, angrily.

"I was a fool, Carey. I was proud of you, until I let my own pride get in the way and make me stupid. I thought I'd go off and join the navy for awhile until

I decided what I wanted to do. Well as soon as I was committed, I knew I wanted to be back here with you, but then they shipped us out, and all this began."

"So why didn't you call us when you got out of prison in Sydney?"

Miranda wished her Mom would drop it. Here was her dad, back from the dead, and she didn't want to hear her parents argue.

"I had no money, not even for a phone call. I tried to borrow some from the embassy, but they wanted proof of identity. They weren't about to risk helping someone who wasn't really a U.S. citizen. I finally got a job as an apprentice builder. The pay wasn't great at first, but I was able to buy a meal before I starved to death. A. J. and I worked together for awhile until he found a pretty Australian girl who took a liking to him. She talked him into leaving Sydney to go work on her father's ranch. I've talked to him a few times, since. He has several children now and loves his life," Barry sighed.

"That doesn't answer your question, does it?" he continued. "Well, I was a coward, once I finally got paid, I bought pen and paper and started writing letters. I'd get about ready to send them, and then I'd think, 'She probably has a fine home and family with someone else by now. If I tell her I'm alive and want her back, what will she think? How will it help her?' Or sometimes, I'd just think, 'I can't let Carey see me like this. I have nothing to offer her. I don't even have decent clothes, or money to buy a ticket out of here.' I'd tear up the letter and throw it away, and the next day, I'd write another one. I finally got good enough at building that I could work on my own and started doing better financially. I decided I'd save, not only enough to get back to the states, but enough to be able to buy a ranch and build you a home when I got here."

"And you thought I'd just be sitting here waiting?" Carey asked.

"No. I was terribly afraid you wouldn't be. I was afraid I was too late a long time ago, and even though I wanted it with all my heart, I was afraid to hope I'd actually get another chance. The longer I put it off, the harder it was to take the chance to call or come or even write a letter.

"And then one night, not long ago, I couldn't sleep, so I went out walking to a hill where I could stare up at the sky, and I saw the biggest, brightest shooting star I've ever seen. All I could think of was, make a wish before it disappears, and I wished to see my wife and child. As soon as I actually put it into words, I thought, well, if that wish is going to come true, I'll have to make it happen. The next day, I gave notice to the people I was building a housing project for. I told them I would finish the house I was building to give them time to find someone else. I took my savings out of the bank, bought an airline ticket, and headed back for the States."

"What day was that, when you wished on the star?" Miranda asked.

"April ninth," he said.

"Shooting Star's birthday," Miranda said, looking at Margot and squeezing her hand.

"You've been through a lot, Barry," Grandpa said. "What are your plans now?"

"Well, Sir," Barry said, uncertainly. "Like I said, I have some money saved. I'd like to buy some land and build on it, but, well, there are a lot of unknowns yet. So I don't know where or when...," his voice trailed off as he looked at Carey.

"Take your time, boy," Grandpa said. "I just wondered if you'd be free to help out around here for awhile until I'm back on my feet again. As you know the work never gets caught up on a dairy farm."

Miranda smiled, but noticed that both Adam and Mom were frowning. Barry smiled and reached out to shake Grandpa's hand.

"Sure, I'd love to. May I start tomorrow morning?" he asked.

"Be here bright and early. Miranda will show you the ropes around the milk barn," Grandpa said.

"Does that mean you're firing me?" Adam asked.

"Why no! It means I'm relieving the women in this family of the chores that have been keeping them on the go from dawn to dusk. You've been doing the feeding and some of the clean up. I'm not taking that job away from you, if you still want it."

"Well, I'd better go, then," Barry said, smiling and tapping on Grandpa's back brace. "It's great to see you, John. I'll enjoy it even more when you're out of that turtle shell."

"Not as much as I will," Grandpa said with a laugh. "Good night, son. I'll see you in the milk barn, bright and early."

"Carey, do you want to walk me out to my truck?" Adam growled as he headed for the door.

"Sure," she said. "I'll get my sweater."

Grandpa and Grandma both helped with the milking in the morning, but soon saw that Miranda and Barry had everything under control.

"I'll go fix breakfast, so Carey can sleep in this morning," Grandma said.

Adam showed up late to do the feeding and Miranda had all the bucket calves fed, and Barry had cleaned the milk barn and fed the feeder steers before he got there. Adam didn't have much to say to either of them and declined when Grandma invited him to breakfast. Barry ate a big plateful of buttermilk pancakes, bacon and eggs.

"That was the best breakfast I've had since I left here, Kathy," he said as he slid his chair back from the table. "Now John, tell me what all needs to be done around here and which jobs are most important."

When there was finally a break in the men's conversation, Miranda interrupted.

"Dad?" she asked, trying out the word, for the first time, "Would you like to go to Shady Hills and see Starlight and Shooting Star?"

"Sure," he began, "as soon as..."

"You run along now," Grandpa ordered. "Mandy has been helping out around here like a trouper. She deserves some time off with her friends and her horses. Please take her, if you don't mind."

"It'll be a pleasure!" Barry exclaimed.

"May I go, too?" asked Margot timidly.

"Sure," said Miranda, taking the younger girl's hand. "Let's go!"

Laurie met Miranda when they pulled up in front of the stable.

"Oh, good, Miranda, you're here. I was going to call you. It's Shooting Star. She looks like a pin cushion! Chris is with her!"

Chapter Seventeen

"What happened?" Miranda asked as they ran to Queen's stall.

But as soon as she opened the door, she could see. Chris sat on the floor, cradling the foal's head in his lap, trying to pull porcupine quills from her nose. Shooting Star pulled back and slipped out of his grasp, every time he got hold of one. There were dozens sticking out of her nostrils, her lip, and chin.

"Here, let me help," Barry said as he pulled a small tool kit from his pocket.

He took out a small pair of scissors and a pair of tweezers and knelt beside Chris.

"Maybe I could take your place and you three kids can help hold her still while I get these things out," he said.

Chris looked at the man in surprise, but moved carefully out from under Shooting Star's head. The foal jumped to her feet. Barry picked her up gently and cradled her in his lap.

"Chris, Laurie," Miranda said, "this is my dad, Barry Stevens."

Laurie and Chris stared at Barry as if they were seeing a ghost. They finally closed their gaping mouths and helped Miranda hold Shooting Star still as Barry carefully clipped the end of each quill. When he gripped each one with the tweezers, and with a quick flick of his wrist, pulled it out, Shooting Star twitched and kicked. Barry carefully looked at the inside of her mouth and found three more, one in her tongue and two inside her lower lip. He pulled those out in the same way. When he was through, he released her, petted her gently for a few moments before she jumped up. Chris opened the door to the paddock and let her return to her worried mother.

"Keep an eye on her," Barry warned. "I think I got them all, but if I left even part of one in, it could get infected. If you see any sign of that, call the vet."

Miranda took her father to see Starlight. She proudly longed her horse and had him perform all the tricks she'd taught him as her father watched. Refusing Dad's help, she saddled him and took him to the track.

"Time us, Dad!" Miranda shouted. "There has never been a faster horse on this track."

When she finally brought Starlight to a stop after running three times around the track, she watched her father's face with apprehension. She wanted him to share her excitement so much it hurt.

"That was incredible!" Barry said, as he walked

up to her, shaking his head. "You are unbelievable, daughter."

He held his arms up to her, and she slid off Starlight's back into them. She lay her head on his shoulder in perfect contentment for several moments before looking into his eyes. When she did, she saw tears.

"What's the matter?" she asked in alarm. "Did I do something wrong?"

"No, I did. I left," he whispered. "Miranda, no matter what your mother decides about marrying Adam, I am going to stay as close as I can to you. I've missed out on way too much of your life, and I will not make that mistake again."

"You mean you'll stay with us?"

"Well, not in the same house, of course. But I'll find a cheap place to rent. Your grandpa needs my help right now. When he gets his brace off and all his strength back, I'll find another job close by. If they move you away from here, I'll follow."

"I don't want to leave here, ever," Miranda said. "Where are you staying?"

"In a hotel over in Three Forks. It makes a long drive back and forth," he said. "Would you like to go with me to look for something closer before time to start the milking?"

"Sure," Miranda said. "Let me tell my friends and Margot where we're going."

"Where should we look?" asked Barry. "I know this little town doesn't have a newspaper."

"There's a bulletin board at the diner and also

at the gas station," Miranda said.

They bought lunch in the diner and checked the bulletin board as they waited to be served. There were no rentals posted, so Barry asked the waitress.

"Yes, Mrs. Mullins has a small apartment that might be available. The science teacher moved out of it as soon as school let out, and as far as I know, she hasn't tried to rent it."

Mrs. Mullins was a kind and jolly old lady who attended every function the school put on, even though she had not had any family attending since her last grandchild graduated fifteen years earlier. She told Barry and Miranda all this and more as she showed them the two small rooms at the back of her house. A few years ago, she told them, she had hired someone to remodel them into a bedroom and kitchenette.

"I'll take it," Barry said. "May I move in tomorrow?"

When Miranda came in from the barn after the milking was done and her father had gone home, she looked for her mother.

"She went out with Adam," Grandma told her. "I'm baby-sitting."

Kort grinned at Miranda as Grandma held him on her lap in the rocking chair.

"He should be going to sleep soon," Grandma said. "But he doesn't seem the least bit sleepy."

"I'll play with him if you want to do something else," Miranda offered. "Where's Margot."

"She went to your room as soon as she got home,

and hasn't come out since. Adam brought her home from Shady Hills when he came to pick up your mother."

Miranda took Kort by the hand and led him to her room. Margot was lying on the bed reading a book.

"How was your day?" Miranda asked.

"Umphh," Margot grunted.

"That bad?"

"No," Margot said, laying her book down. "It was great until my father came to take me home."

"Not ready to go, yet, huh?"

"It wasn't that," Margot said, sitting up and looking at Miranda.

Her eyes were red from crying.

"What happened?"

"Elliot and I were in the hay loft, talking. All of a sudden, there was Adam at the top of the ladder yelling at us."

"Yelling at you? What for?"

"That's what I want to know. He told us to both come down that minute, and he didn't want to catch us up there again."

"Why?" asked Miranda.

"That's what I asked him. He just said he didn't want any back talk."

"Good grief! Did you ever find out why he was mad?" Miranda asked.

"I don't have a clue. Elliot asked him if we'd done something wrong. He said it ever so politely, and he got the same answer I got," Margot said with a sniffle. "On the way home, I asked him why he was mad, because we didn't do anything. He just said he didn't want me to be close friends with Elliot."

"Why not? There isn't anything wrong with Elliot. He is the sweetest, best little kid I know," Miranda said. "Well, you are too, but you know what I mean."

"We were talking about our dads, but I don't think he heard us. If he did, that would probably make him mad," Margot said.

"Did he ever give a reason?"

"He said because we wouldn't be here long. He said that after the wedding we're all going back to California."

"What wedding?" Miranda shouted. "They can't get married now. Mom's married to Dad, and Dad isn't dead even if Adam wishes he was!"

Kort looked up from the book he was playing with on the floor.

"Manda mad?" he asked.

"Sorry, Kort. I didn't mean to..." Miranda began. "Hey, Kort what are you doing? You aren't supposed to tear the pages out. No, no. Here, play with this toy doggie."

She picked up the book and the torn pages as she listened to Margot.

"He said that Carey can get an annulment and it won't take very long."

"What if Mom doesn't want one!"

"He thinks she does. He says he can't wait to get married and get out of this god-forsaken country. That's how he said it."

Miranda sat in silence, fighting tears of anger and desperation as she watched Kort play.

"Will you go with us?" Margot asked.

"Are you kidding? I'd rather be homeless than live with Adam Barber."

"You have a choice," Margot said quietly as tears flowed down her cheeks.

"I'm sorry, Margot," Miranda said, putting her arm around the smaller girl. "We'll talk them into letting you stay here with Grandma and Grandpa. No," she said, changing her mind. "We've got to do better than that. We've got to make sure they don't get married. I really think Mom still loves Dad."

"Then my dad would leave and make me go with him," Margot said, sobbing. "That would be worse."

"Maybe not," Miranda said, knowing she didn't sound very reassuring.

Miranda lay awake a long time after everyone else in the house had gone to sleep. When she heard her mother come in, she got up and followed her into her back porch bedroom.

"What are you doing up so late?" Mom asked.

"I couldn't sleep," Miranda said. "What time is it?"

"Around midnight. Where's Kort?"

"He's in my bed, all snuggled up with Margot. They both look so comfortable, I think we should just leave him there."

Mom smiled as she sat down at her dressing

table to take off her make up. "Okay by me. If he wakes up in the night, and you can't handle him, come and get me."

"Mom, are you going to marry Adam?"

"That's still the plan, I guess."

"But you're married. What about Dad?"

"I haven't looked into what the law says about that. I've been single for twelve years, Miranda. He was legally dead."

"But he's not dead. He's wonderful, Mom. I don't see how you can even like Adam compared to him."

Mom didn't answer.

"Adam said you were getting an annulment."

"He suggested that. I don't know if it's even necessary," Mom said. "Did he tell you that?"

"He told Margot. Mom, do you love Adam?"

"Oh, Miranda," Mom said, turning to face her, "I don't know what I feel. I made a promise to Adam, and I meant it when I accepted his proposal. Sometimes when I'm with him, I'm not so sure. But I don't know what would happen to Margot if I don't marry him. And I do know I've fallen in love with her."

"I don't think Adam even likes her. He's mean to her, Mom."

"Miranda, you don't know that. You have had it so easy, you think if anyone disciplines a child, he's being mean to her."

"I know how bad he makes her feel. My dad doesn't make me feel that way!"

"Would you stop comparing the two?" Mom

said, raising her voice. "I can't forget how much your dad hurt me — hurt both of us. What he did was unforgivable, yet you are willing to take him back in a heartbeat, as if you hadn't suffered most of your life with the knowledge that your father left before you were born because he didn't want you."

"That's not true. That's what I thought, but...," Miranda began to cry. "So that's the reason you never wanted me. You think it's my fault he left!"

"No, I don't. Miranda I didn't mean it like that."

But Miranda ran to the bathroom, slammed the door and locked it. She slumped onto the floor, buried her head between her knees and sobbed.

Chapter Eighteen

Miranda was out of the house long before her mother got up the next morning. She even beat Grandpa to the barn and had the milkers put together and the first six cows in the barn by the time her dad arrived to help with the morning milking.

"Good morning, Miranda, daughter of mine," he said with a smile.

"Morning," Miranda answered shortly. "Everything's ready. I'm going to go feed."

Adam hadn't been coming in the mornings since Barry arrived. Miranda didn't care. She'd rather do the work herself than to have Adam around.

When the steers were fed, Miranda went back to get milk for the bucket fed calves. Then she made sure they had plenty of water and a little grain in their feeders. She did her share of the clean up and then went to the hay barn. She didn't feel like talking to anyone, least of all her mother or father. She sat with her arms around Little Brother, trying to sort out the avalanche of feelings that had seemed to knock her off her feet.

"Anything you'd care to talk about?"

Miranda was startled by her dad's quiet voice. "How did you find me?"

"Wasn't hard. When I used to live here with your mom, this is where I'd come when I wanted to be alone and think."

"Did you think about how much you hated having a baby?"

"I thought about that and a lot of other things," he said, as he sat down next to her. "How ill prepared I was. What a mistake Carey had made when she married me. How I didn't want to be a dead beat dad, living off my wife's family."

"So it's true. You left because of me!"

"Not entirely. I used you as an excuse to not face up to responsibility. I was scared and I ran. I'm not proud of it. I've regretted it since the first day I did it. You don't have to forgive me, Miranda, but I am truly sorry. I can't blame your mother if she never forgives me. But I will spend the rest of my life trying to make it up to both of you if I get the chance."

Miranda had expected him to deny it. She wouldn't have believed him if he had. But he admitted he had left because of her, so she believed him when he said he was sorry. She leaned into his arms and cried the tears she'd been holding in all morning.

"I've got good news," Grandma said when she

picked Miranda up at Shady Hills the next Monday.

"What?"

"This may be the last day Grandpa has to wear his body brace. He has a doctor's appointment tomorrow. He's been getting better every day. Last night he slept through the night without having to take pain pills," Grandma said, smiling from ear to ear.

"Hooray! We've got to celebrate. May we have a big dinner for him when he gets home? I'll make his favorite cake. We'll invite Dad. Grandpa loves to visit with him and he hasn't come around the house much the last few days."

"Sounds good to me," Grandma said. "I bet your Mom will help with the meal. Better not invite Adam, though. It might be awkward."

"No, I think we should!" Miranda exclaimed. "I'm sure Mom will want him to be there, and Grandpa won't mind."

"Are you sure?" Grandma asked, looking at her in surprise. "I thought you'd jump at any excuse to keep Adam away."

But Miranda had an idea. The more times Mom saw the two men together, the more she had to see which one was the best. Sooner or later she'd surely realize she didn't love Adam.

Grandpa's appointment was at one o'clock, so Miranda planned the meal for three thirty. That should give them time to get back from Bozeman, and they could still finish eating before milking time. Miranda got out a recipe book and looked up burnt sugar cake. It looked awfully complicated, but she followed the directions as carefully as she could, and with a little help from her mother, baked it successfully.

Mom agreed to make rolls and put a roast in the oven. Miranda was peeling potatoes when the phone rang.

"Would you get that, Margot?" Mom called from the pantry where she was on a stool looking for a jar of chokecherry jelly, Grandpa's favorite.

"It's for you. Long distance," Miranda heard Margot tell her mother.

Mom climbed off the stool, handed the jelly to Miranda, and took the phone.

"Yes, why he's doing just great. Growing like a weed, and talking. I think he says a half dozen new words everyday," Mom said, as Miranda tried to guess who it was.

Kort's mother was overseas again. Miranda didn't think she'd be calling unless it was an emergency, and it didn't sound like one.

"You're what? When? And you're moving to Milan? But it's so sudden." Mom sat down and her face turned pale. "What about Kort?"

There was a long silence. Miranda stopped working and watched her mom intently.

"Are you sure about this?" Mom asked. "Of course I would! You know how much I love him. It would kill me to have him leave, but you can't change your mind later."

Miranda was puzzled. Mom finally hung up the phone and turned toward Miranda and Margot looking dazed.

"Come sit down in the living room, girls. I have something to tell you."

They sat together on the couch and Miranda reached for Margot's hand as she stared at Mom.

"You know Kort's mother is a model and travels all over the world," she began.

Both girls nodded.

"Well, she says she has fallen in love. She is engaged to be married — tomorrow!"

"Tomorrow. Why so soon?"

"I guess she's afraid the man, a very rich, very handsome designer, will change his mind. She plans to sell her house in California and live in Milan."

"Oh, you won't have a job anymore," Miranda said. "Or does she want you to go to Milan to take care of Kort there?"

"No. She wants me to take care of him here."

"What do you mean?" asked Miranda.

"She hasn't told her fiance that she has a baby. She doesn't want him to know! She said, 'He's not very fond of kids, and I don't think he'd marry me if he knew about Kort.' So she wants to let me adopt him, if I will."

"She's just giving her baby away, for a man?" Miranda couldn't believe her ears. "What kind of mother would do that?"

"Well, she hasn't been around him much in his whole life. She has always traveled and left him with me or the nanny before me. She's very young and her career has always been more important than anything else, including Kort."

"So you'll do it, won't you?" asked Margot.

"Of course, if she actually goes through with it and makes everything legal. I can't have her coming back and trying to take him away from me later."

"What about the house in California? You don't have a place to live!"

"No, I don't," Mom said quietly. "I've got to get all of Kort's and my things moved out of the California mansion before the end of next month. That's when Lorna is coming back with her husband to sell it and decide what to do with all of her things."

The three of them sat and talked about the strange turn of events and what the future would hold, when they heard a car pull into the driveway.

"Oh no!" Miranda exclaimed, "They're here and I don't have the potatoes on to cook yet."

A knock sounded at the door. Miranda turned to open it, but Margot got there first.

"Hope I'm not too early," Barry said, stepping into the dining room.

"You're not early," Miranda said. "We're just late. We got to talking and didn't get the potatoes on in time."

"Is there anything I can do to help," he asked. "I'll set the table, unless there's something else you want me to do first."

"We'll pressure cook the potatoes, and I'll make the gravy while Miranda makes salad," Mom said. "Setting the table would be a great help. Use the good china, and thank you."

When Barry finished setting the table, he made

punch and then started putting the relish plates, butter, and jellies on the table. By the time Grandma and Grandpa arrived, everything was ready. Barry heard their car and went out to walk Grandpa to the house.

"Grandpa," Miranda said, kissing him on the cheek. "You look great without your turtle shell. How does it feel?"

"Free! The doctor says the bones are all healed. I'll be able to do all the chores now."

"We'll see about that," Grandma said. "I don't want you to overdo it and end up flat on your back again."

Mom put a bowl of steaming mashed potatoes on the table and looked out the window.

"I don't know why Adam isn't here yet, but I guess we'd better start without him, or everything will be cold."

By the time everyone had filled their plates, Adam walked in.

"Well, am I that late?" he asked when he saw they were starting to eat.

"We've barely started," Mom said, standing up and pulling out a chair for him. "Come sit beside me."

In a few minutes, Kort began to cry as he woke up from his afternoon nap.

"I'll get him, Mom," Miranda said.

"Thank you, Miranda," Mom said. "I've got some news to tell before Miranda brings Kort to the table. She already knows." Mom paused and took a deep breath. "I got a strange phone call..." Miranda couldn't hear the rest.

"Hi, little Kort! Your new mommy is telling the happy news about you. Oh, are you ever soaked. Let's get you washed up and into a dry diaper and clean clothes."

When Miranda walked back toward the dining room, she heard her mother saying.

"And so, if all goes as I hope it does, Kort is going to be my child."

"That's outrageous, Carey!" Adam exclaimed. "You just agreed without taking time to think it through? Why didn't you talk it over with me first?"

Miranda stopped. She didn't think Kort should hear this.

"What is there to talk about?" Mom asked. "Lorna said she would not keep her baby. She has relatives who she thinks would keep him if I won't, but he doesn't even know them. Do you think I'd let him go to strangers?"

"What about the money? You're going from getting a healthy salary and an expense allowance for taking care of him, to having no income and all the extra expenses of raising a kid," Adam argued.

"I'm sure we'll manage," she said.

Miranda turned and hurried back into the bedroom.

"Kortie eat!" the toddler protested with a howl.

"Okay, okay!" Miranda said, turning toward the dining room again.

"Let's make a toast," Grandpa said when he saw them, "To Kort, our new grandson. May his life be as long, happy, and blest as mine has been."

Miranda sat Kort in the highchair which Mom had placed at the corner of the table between her and Adam. Mom handed him a plate of food and a glass of milk. Kort smiled from ear to ear and reached for the milk. It slipped out of his chubby hands and landed in Adam's lap.

Chapter Nineteen

"Blast it all!" Adam yelled, jumping to his feet and slamming the empty milk glass down hard on the tray of Kort's highchair. "Watch what you're doing, you little brat! If you'd slow down, you wouldn't always be making a mess!"

Kort burst into tears.

"Adam, for heaven's sake! It was an accident. What's the matter with you?" Mom exclaimed as she took Kort from his chair and held him close.

"Me?" Adam asked, as if he couldn't believe she was mad at him. "I'm soaked to the skin in cold, sticky milk, and you wonder why I'm upset?"

"Don't you ever talk to a child like that again!" Mom said. "I don't care if you're choking on milk, you can't punish our children for an accident."

"Our children! I didn't sign up for supporting a family that includes a baby and a stay at home mom. You'd better reconsider this whole thing before you sign any papers, Carey."

"I have reconsidered, Adam. I can see quite clearly that it would be a mistake to marry a man who thinks more of his money than he does his family," Mom said very quietly. "Miranda told me you don't like kids, and I see that she was right. Well I love them, and I couldn't live with a man who didn't."

"Are you calling off our engagement?" Adam asked in surprise.

Mom pulled the diamond ring from her finger and gave it to Adam.

"Yes, I am. Take this and get out of this house."

"Margot," Adam said, as he started for the door, "come with me."

"I don't think that's a good idea, right now, do you?" Grandpa asked. "Come back after you've cooled down."

Adam glared at Grandpa, but didn't argue. He picked up his hat and walked out, slamming the door behind him.

"Oh, Dad, I'm so sorry to spoil your dinner," Mom said, as Kort struggled to get down from her arms.

"That's all right, Carey. I'm fine." Grandpa said with a smile. "Would you pass me some more of that roast beef? You cooked it just right!"

"Margot, are you all right?" Miranda asked as she climbed into bed that night.

"I'm scared," Margot answered so quietly that Miranda could barely hear her.

"Scared of what?"

"My dad. I'm afraid he'll take me away and not let anyone know where to find me."

"He'll have to deal with Grandpa, Mom, and Grandma first. I don't think he has the guts to do that."

"I don't want to go to Shady Hills tomorrow. Would you tell Elliot I'm sorry I couldn't come?"

Grandma had to stop at Bergman's general store for a new pitchfork handle. Miranda went in with her to see if Christopher wanted to go with them to Shady Hills. Laurie had gone to Butte with her mother.

"Oh, good morning, Andrea," Grandma said. "How are you? I haven't seen you since your accident."

Miranda looked up to see Mrs. Meredith at the check out stand. Mr. Bergman was ringing up her purchases.

"Hello Kathy. I'm fine, thanks to you and your little granddaughter. Where is she? I'd like to thank her again."

"This is my granddaughter, Miranda."

"No, I mean the one with the pretty brown curls and sweet smile; the one who helped me and was so polite."

"Oh, you mean Laurie Langley, Miranda's best friend. Yes, she is a sweetheart. She comes from a very good family, so I guess one would expect her to be that way."

"Langley? She's not related..." Mrs. Meredith stammered as her face turned red. "I mean, I don't believe I know her family. Are they new?"

"Her father is the sixth grade teacher at the school. You may have met her mother at the garden club. You're a member of that aren't you?"

"Oh, that Langley."

It looked to Miranda as if a door closed in Mrs. Meredith's face, as she looked down and began fumbling through her purse.

"They've been a wonderful addition to our community since they came here. Mr. Langley is the man who saved little Billy Smythe from their burning barn last year. He's one of the best teachers our school has ever had, in my opinion," Grandma said.

"I wouldn't know," Mrs. Meredith mumbled.

"Andrea, I wish you could get to know them. Have you heard of the watercolor lessons that are going to be given at the Langley's home? She's having a professional come in and teach. It would be a lovely opportunity to get to know the family. You'll see why Laurie has turned out to be such a well behaved and caring young lady."

Grandma's tone had changed from light to sincerely caring. How could anyone resist?

"I don't think I'll have time," the woman said.

"Well, I'll tell Laurie you were asking about her. She'll be glad to know you thought she was helpful."

"You sure told her!" Miranda said as they drove to Shady Hills.

"Well, that wasn't my intention," Grandma said. "I'm afraid I was a little hard on her. You can't win friends by alienating them with ridicule."

"You didn't do that!" Miranda exclaimed.

"Are you sure? I'm afraid I was being a little insincere when I went on about how wonderful the Langleys are."

"But they are!"

"I know. I didn't say anything that I don't believe with my whole heart. But I pretended I didn't know that she has chosen to shun them. And I do know that. I know it, and I think it's wrong, but I'm not sure that I used the most tactful approach."

"Gram! You didn't say anything bad. It wouldn't matter whether you screamed in her face and called her stupid or kissed her feet and asked her nicely, she'd still hate the Langleys for no reason."

"You're right," Grandma said with a sigh. "I just didn't feel very proud of myself. I saw she was embarrassed, and I just kept rubbing it in."

"Maybe it'll get her to thinking."

Grandpa insisted on coming to the barn the next morning, though everyone told him he could celebrate by sleeping in. He said he felt fine and wanted to get back to "full speed." He and Barry talked and joked, but never mentioned the incident at the table, at least not while Miranda was in the barn with them.

When she was bucket feeding milk to the calves, Grandpa came out to watch her. He got there just in time to see one of the bigger calves butt the bucket just as she was taking it from him. It caught her off balance and she fell backward on her seat.

"Hey, you little bully! That's no way to treat my number one helper!" Grandpa shouted.

Miranda got up laughing and gave her grandfather a hug.

"It's so nice to see you without that brace, Grandpa."

"You have no idea how nice it is to be free of it. It feels kind of funny, though, like I forgot my overalls or something."

"Grandpa, what will we do if Adam tries to take Margot away from us?"

"Well, legally there isn't much of anything we can do. I'd sure do my best to talk him out of it, though. I don't think he wants to be saddled with a child, not even his own," Grandpa said.

"But he might take her just to get revenge on Mom," Miranda said.

It was almost noon when Dad took Miranda to Shady Hills. Elliot ran to meet them, looking disappointed when he saw that Margot wasn't with them.

"Is Margot gone, too?" he asked, his eyes wide with fear.

"Too? What do you mean? Who else is gone?" Miranda asked.

"Adam. He loaded all of his furniture and clothes in his camper and pulled out about an hour ago," Elliot said. "Did he come get Margot?"

"He hadn't when we left," Miranda said. "I think I'll call home and make sure."

Margot answered. No, Adam hadn't been there. She was going to hide if he drove in, she said.

"Here comes Grandfather," Elliot said. "I think

he wants to talk to you, Mr. Stevens."

"Good morning, Mr. Taylor," Dad said, reaching out to shake the old man's hand.

"I have a proposition for you, young man," Mr. Taylor said as he withdrew his hand from Barry's firm grip. "I just lost my help, and I thought I'd ask you if you'd be interested in a job. Are you? The pay may not be what you are used to, but it's pretty good for this part of the country."

"And what kind of work would I be doing?"

"General ranch work. A lot of feeding in the winter time, but mostly working with Higgins to manage the horses. I actually have three operations around here. I take care of the paper work, Higgins decides what needs to be done next, and you'd be in charge of seeing that it gets carried out."

"What three operations?"

"I raise and breed both quarter horses and Thoroughbreds. I also have a string of dude horses; horses I rent out to people. That helps pay the bills, but my main interest is the race horses, and I need a good trainer for that."

"I don't have any experience with horses," Barry said.

Miranda, who was listening eagerly to every word, wished he wouldn't discourage Mr. Taylor. She thought it would be great if he took the job.

"It's been my experience that the best workers are those willing to learn, not the ones who think they already know it all."

Like Adam, Miranda thought.

"Well, Sir, I'm willing to learn, and I am a good worker. There's just one condition I'd have to work out first," Barry said.

"And what would that be?" Mr. Taylor asked.

"I'll be spending some of my time on the Greene place. For one thing I'm going to build a house over there. I think I can whip it out pretty fast on the weekends and evenings and maybe a few full days while the weather is nice. I would work around the pressing needs of your schedule," Dad said.

"You're going to build a house on the dairy?" Miranda asked as they rode home that evening.

"Your grandpa asked me to. He wants a nice place for Carey to stay with her family. The little farm house is getting awfully crowded, as you know. So it will be your house, too, unless you prefer to stay in your old room."

In a few weeks the house was already taking shape. Miranda walked over to investigate when she got off the school bus the first day of school. Mom and Dad were standing together in the doorway when Miranda walked up behind them. They didn't hear her coming.

"But how do I know I can trust you not to walk out on us again?" Mom asked.

"How could you know that about anyone? The fact that I did it once, doesn't mean I'll do it again. As I see it, it's a guarantee that I won't. I may be hard headed, Carey, but I learn from my mistakes. I spent many years regretting that I left. Do you think I'm dumb enough to repeat that mistake?" Dad said. "Besides, I have several more reasons to stay. Some very weighty anchors."

"What?" asked Mom.

"Miranda. I cherish my daughter. I promised I will spend the rest of my life as near to her as I can. You can believe I mean it. And little Kort. He's adorable and I'd like to help you raise him. And you. I'm crazy about you, Carey. I want to be with you and help you with these kids. I want to help you fight Adam for custody of Margot, if it ever comes to that."

Miranda, ashamed for eavesdropping, turned to leave, but she tripped on a rock and fell.

"Miranda!" Mom said. "Are you okay? Did you just get here?"

"I brought the mail," Miranda said, trying to hide her embarrassment as she got to her feet. "There's a letter for you, Mom."

Mom took the envelope. It was post marked Chicago, but had no return address.

"It's from Adam," she finally said. "He says he isn't settled yet. He wants me to keep Margot until he has a permanent place for her. Knowing him, that might be never."

"Well, I don't understand Adam, but I think Margot is better off here," Dad said."

"Well, back to the house plans," Mom said. "I think we should make the master bedroom a little bigger. I want you to share it with me. But first, I want to have the wedding I was planning with a few changes."

"Like the groom?"

"Yes," Mom whispered with a smile.

"And the dresses?" Miranda asked.

"Yes, that, too. Maybe we'll have the wedding in the mountains and let everyone wear jeans." Mom said with a laugh.

As if Miranda wasn't even there, Barry pulled Carey close and kissed her.

Miranda, red faced but smiling, ran to tell Margot the good news

If you enjoyed *Miranda and Starlight, Starlight's Courage, Starlight, Star Bright,* and *Starlight's Shooting Star* you'll want to read the exciting continuation of the saga of Miranda and her beloved horse, Starlight.
Books 5 and 6 will be available in 2004.

Happy Reading and Riding to You!

$9.00 (U.S.) per book plus $2.00 shipping and handling for one and $.50 for each additional book.

To order, send check or money order to:

 Raven Publishing
P.O. Box 2885
Norris, MT 59745
USA

For more information, e-mail:
info@ravenpublishing.net
Phone: *406-685-3545*
Toll Free: 866-685-3545
Fax: *406-685-3599*
Order online at:
www.ravenpublishing.net